PRAISE FOR *COIL QUAKE RIFT*

"*Coil Quake Rift* is a cinematic, contemplative, reality-bending page-turner deepened by its vivid Los Angeles setting and its intriguing questions about multiple universes and the afterlife."

— **Andromeda Romano-Lax,**
author of *Annie and the Wolves*

"*Coil Quake Rift* grapples fearlessly with the inescapable motif of the apocalypse that haunts our century. With kinetic, vibrant prose and visionary point of view, Elias has crafted a stunning novel with a mesmerizing plot and provocative existential themes. A marvelous book that adds to the rich literary tradition of Los Angeles disaster narratives, *Coil Quake Rift* reminds us the apocalypse is both personal and collective. Just like the rift that has opened in Elias's depiction of Venice Beach, this book will open a fissure in your mind and in your heart."

— **Alistair McCartney,**
author of *The Disintegrations* and
The End of the World Book

"A haunting philosophical thriller, Nathan Elias's debut novel *Coil Quake Rift* more than fulfills the promise of his 2020 short story collection, *The Reincarnations*. It's frankly dizzying to think that, in just a couple of books, Elias has proven himself that rarest of authors: a sci-fi master who loves people, their faults and foibles, their wishes and dreams."

— **Christopher Clancy,**
author of *We Take Care of Our Own*

PRAISE FOR *THE REINCARNATIONS: STORIES*

"Fast-moving and deeply felt stories, sharply envisioned and lit with humor and compassion. Nathan Elias writes like he's lived a thousand lives."

— **Ben Loory,**
author of *Tales of Falling and Flying*

"Nathan Elias's fearless debut collection is a genre-defying labyrinth of loss and heartache...These deft stories signal a tremendous talent in capturing what it means to be human in this or other realities."

— **Sequoia Nagamatsu,**
author of *Where We Go When All We Were Is Gone*

"Nathan Elias writes about the world—both as we know it and as we hadn't yet thought to imagine it—through a singular, deeply compassionate, lens, showing us both its monstrousness and its beauty."

— **Gayle Brandeis,**
author of *Many Restless Concerns*

"*Twin Peaks* meets Raymond Carver...The texture of Elias's gritty speculation deserves to be experienced in full."

— **Pedro Ponce,**
Heavy Feather Review

"These stories focus on the aftermath of catastrophe as characters stumble in their attempts to process loss... *The Reincarnations* helps us make sense of the painful and outrageous in our lives."

— **Sean Kinch,**
Nashville Scene via *Chapter 16: Humanities Tennessee*

"These stories are imaginative and magical, but they also never lose the touch of humanity that makes them feel so universal."

— **Bradley Sides,**
Southern Review of Books

COIL QUAKE RIFT

A NOVEL

NATHAN ELIAS

First Montag Press E-Book and Paperback Original Edition December 2021

Montag Press ISBN: 978-1-957010-00-7
Design © 2021 Amit Dey

Montag Press Team:

Cover Art: Peter Selgin
Author Photo: A. Milano
Editor: Kathryn Sargeant
Managing Director: Charlie Franco

A Montag Press Book
www.montagpress.com
Montag Press
777 Morton Street, Unit B
San Francisco CA 94129 USA

Printed & Digitally Originated in the United States of America
10 9 8 7 6 5 4 3 2 1

For Alexi, again and always.

Books by
Nathan Elias

The Reincarnations

Coil Quake Rift

"It is said that fact is sometimes stranger than fiction, and nowhere is this more true than in the case of black holes."

–Stephen Hawking,
Into a Black Hole

"Now through the noiseless throng their way they bend, And both with pain the rugged road ascend."

–Ovid, *Metamorphoses*

COIL QUAKE RIFT

PROLOGUE

TIFFANY

Tiffany climbed the stepladder and tightened the rope around her neck. Six years, she thought. He has what's coming to him. A wave of calm washed over her. Though she was but moments from kicking away the stepladder, a smirk of revenge punctuated her face. He would not be able to go a day without suffocating beneath the weight of his betrayal, and with RIFT completed *if my calculations are correct*, he would, presumably, be unable to escape the city, forced to confront after death his choices from life *the divine brink before which I now stand, awaiting the beginning of infinity*. And how could she not feel the anchor of memory pulling her down? Hundreds—no, thousands—of wasted moments filling the staves of her mind like music notes, the composition adding up to the short sonata of her life. Flooded by the downpour of memories, she considered loosening the rope, stepping down, and forgetting him forever. But the thought of him with another woman surged through her, blinded her with raging envy. No, the only way she'd come down would be in Knox's arms *your final chance to hold me*. Besides, she'd already launched RIFT; soon the reionizer would begin to accelerate; the copper core she installed into the carbine reactor would emit its pale yellow light, humming quietly with the slightest pulse of electricity; the code she'd written—mostly from memory with few improvisations in the linearity of letters, digits, and symbols—would soon automatize, propelling the gateway with electromagnetic radiation; it wouldn't be until after she was in the ground that the gravitational effects of the rift would begin to take hold. She'd planned the event horizon—the point of no return—to expand its immutable surface over a carefully chosen geographic coordinate; it would take time—several hundred days—but when the ground began to shake he would know she had returned *do you believe in life after death? Would you again Eurydice receive, should fate her quick-spun thread of life re-weave?* She heard the dog whimpering through the two doors separating them. She wondered if the dog sensed her intentions, if he would feel her absence when all the light escaped her body *some experts dispute whether atoms are part of who we are, that atoms are in our bodies forever until becoming carbon dioxide—food for future organisms; the calcium and phosphorous in our bones will become part of plant life; the helium that is left of us will defy Earth's gravity and drift into outer space. But what do these experts know of the soul?* She had been researching quantum field theory—dark matter and energy—and the existence of spirit particles for years, enough time to separate emotional attachments to death from the science of it. *There is but a hairline dividing life and death.* One jolt of the leg was all it would take to leave her suspended from the beam in the ceiling. She'd tested the rope and ligature point with free weights *the noose, or as Virgil put it, the coil of unbecoming death, is the purest way to do it—reliant entirely on mass* with the precision she'd have used with any experiment. *I wonder if I led you to her, if your union was my part to play in this go-around. What defines a person's life? Achievements? Experiences? Or is it the sum of our actions?* It was the elegance of asphyxiation that had appealed to her; it had been the thought of so much wasted time *not only my years with you, years in which I believed I'd found my soul mate, but also what I chose to study—the black holes. If RIFT succeeds, maybe my life's work won't have been for nothing; but if it fails, then what purpose will my countless hours of research and experiments have served?* that made her decide to end it, hoping there would be another chance on the other side. The science had led her to publish academic work about what existed beyond the vortices of black holes; like the ocean's tide, black holes, she learned, were in flux with gravity, could be swayed by the moon *how convenient that you chose to elope on the spring equinox—a coincidence, or did you intend for her to be your new beginning? What did you expect would happen to the past when you chose a new present? There is a line in the Emerald Tablet you should think about: "All which exists is only another form of that which exists not."* She knew her family was only a phone call away, that her parents would have given anything to hear from her at that moment. *Choices make us who we are.* But nothing could have made Tiffany dial them. *The choices alone procreate our experience, our world.* She closed her eyes, *This is not goodbye, my love.* drew a breath, *Choose wisely.* and kicked the stepladder out from under her.

PART 1

POWERLESS

THEY WERE HAVING make-up sex when the lights went out.

With the tremors that interrupted their argument still fresh in Margot's mind—the shaking walls of their Hollywood apartment, the picture frames smashing to the floor—she rolled to face her husband and put a hand to her stomach. Knox held her. "Calm," he said. "Stay calm. It's only a reaction to the earthquake."

In the fresh darkness of their bedroom, she considered the power outage trivial compared to what was happening between them. She thought back to before the tremors and the argument, when he was busy preparing their anniversary dinner and she was busy hiding in the bathroom, taking the test.

She'd felt weak upon seeing the blue plus sign, and she wrapped the stick in toilet paper and tossed it in the wastebasket. From there she had stepped out onto the balcony and sat before the canvas she had been working on for days: a view of The Capitol Records building stacked high like a pile of vinyl to the left, and Broadway Hollywood on the right, with Vine Street running straight down the center of the canvas, separating the two buildings. Under the night sky, traffic lights formed streaks of red, yellow, and bone white. She'd noticed Lane, their Golden Retriever, at her feet, wagging his tail, begging to be petted. The breeze felt cool against her skin.

"So lifelike," Knox had said.

She hadn't realized he'd come up behind her.

"Dinner's almost ready."

He kissed the top of her head and went inside. How long before she had to tell him? Could she make that decision alone?

"Be there in a minute," she said.

She picked up a Number #2 brush and dipped it in a blob of alizarin. A single stroke transformed the sky from serene to ominous. If she were to do it without telling him, it would have to be soon. Her first, and only, miscarriage happened four months before she had met Knox. It came eight weeks into her term. That left twenty-eight days for history to repeat itself. Unless she took matters into her own hands.

In the kitchen, she found Knox setting the table, humming to the instrumental jazz playing on his cell phone. "I've been thinking about Florida," he said. "I can't wait to meet your family, have a real ceremony. We deserve that much." She sat down. He poured them each a glass of chardonnay, then raised his glass.

"To us," he said, "We've been through a lot this year. Even when the odds were against us, we pulled through. I look forward to many, many more years with you, Margot."

"So cheesy," she said. "I married a walking greeting card."

"I am a strong believer in embracing cheesiness."

It was true, and one of the many things she loved about him. But, as he leaned in to kiss her, it occurred to her that this was also the anniversary of Knox leaving Tiffany, whose suicide followed a week later. Margot took a mouthful of wine and forced a smile. "Happy anniversary."

During the appetizers, she tried to be engaging when Knox brought up the new documentary project he'd started working on. Something about the anomalistic nature of Hollywood Boulevard and shooting a long, static take on a busy afternoon. Her mind, however, was mostly on the test, until, halfway through the main course, Knox asked her how things were at the school.

She'd drawn a blank, had to make something up about recent parent funding, planning an entire month on glass-blowing. "You'd be surprised how much goes into it," she said. "Shaping the material, heating the kiln, annealing the glass."

She felt the buzz of the wine. Without realizing it, she'd drunk most of the bottle. Probably not the smartest choice, considering her condition. Oh, well, she thought, emptying the last drops into her glass. It would help her tell him about the test. In her mind she composed different sentences, calculating how they would sound were she to speak them. Sentence A: I'm pregnant, but I don't want to have a baby. Sentence B: I'm pregnant but I can't have a baby because there's something I haven't told you. Sentence C: We need to talk. In the middle of composing Sentence D, she looked up to find Knox gone. Moments later she heard his muffled yells coming from down the hall. He was reprimanding their dog for tearing through the bathroom trash. That's when she realized she had left the bathroom door wide open, and the trashcan unemptied. Damn, she thought.

"Margot?" He'd held the test with his fingertips like a dead mouse. "What is this?"

"Sit down," she said.

"You're pregnant."

"Please." She indicated the sofa.

He obeyed, setting the test strip on the coffee table.

"When were you going to tell me?"

"Tonight," she said. "After the dishes."

"You've been drinking."

"Only a little," she said. "It won't hurt."

He looked at the empty bottle, and then back at her.

"Right," he said. "Well, this is amazing news. I want to hold you."

"Wait. I need to think."

"What is there to think about?"

"Please," she'd said, holding out her hand. She closed her eyes. "There's something I should have told you when we first got together. When I was with Jason, I got pregnant."

It had been so long since she'd had to cope.

She'd hoped this new life would bury the old one.

What a mistake, she thought.

"And you lost it," Knox said.

She opened her eyes and looked at him. He stared at the test. Lane cried from the balcony. She exhaled, trying to force memories from her mind: bleeding, the ambulance, the curettage.

"Why didn't you tell me?"

She cleared her throat.

"Because of Tiffany." She looked around for another bottle of wine that could help her forget the role she played in the woman's undoing. "I might have told you. But after what happened, everything else seemed so insignificant."

She noticed Knox shiver at the mention of Tiffany.

"I want to know these things about you," he said.

"I thought I could forget."

"You can't erase the past."

He'd said the same thing when he caught her deleting photos of Tiffany from his computer.

You can't erase the past, Margot.

"I know that," she said. "But that doesn't mean we have to live with constant reminders."

Knox stood. He paused before embracing her. Margot bit her lip and let him hold her.

"We can get through this," he said. "Together."

Her face against his chest, she fought back tears.

"I'm too scared," she said.

"Scared of what?"

She backed away, looked into his eyes.

"Of losing another child."

He touched her face.

"What makes you think you will?"

"I don't want to find out."

He lowered his hand.

"What are you saying?"

Margot turned away, breaking eye contact.

"Was Tiffany ever pregnant?" she asked.

Knox cocked his head. "I don't think so."

"Then you don't know what it feels like."

"Maybe I don't," he said. "But I can empathize with you, right?"

"Jason didn't."

Knox scoffed. Margot couldn't believe she'd actually said that.

"I'm not Jason."

"No, you're not."

They'd stood for a few minutes without speaking. Margot's heart pounded.

"I don't want you to do what you might be thinking about doing," he said. "You know that, right?"

"And why not?"

He stared at her. She saw his face go flush. "Have you done it before?"

"No," she said. "I was only pregnant once."

"You had a miscarriage," he said. "I understand that."

"No," she said. "You don't understand. I couldn't handle it."

"Handle what?"

"Another unexpected loss." She realized how paradoxical she sounded. "It's easier for me if I can control it."

"Sweetheart," he said. "You can't control everything in life."

"I know that. I'm not a child."

"Look," he said and reached for her shoulder. "I know you're upset, but we have to talk about this one way or another."

She recoiled.

"No. We don't have to talk about it. I'm capable of making this decision by myself, thanks."

"Now you're acting like a child."

Maybe so, she thought, wishing she could eat her words. Still, she kept her back to him.

Lane scratched at the screen door, whining to come inside.

Margot said, "Can you please walk him?"

"If you make that decision," Knox said, keeping his voice steady, "I'm not sure I could handle it."

Just like Jason couldn't handle it, she wanted to say, but stopped herself.

"Fine," she'd said instead. "I'll take him." She'd bumped Knox's shoulder while trying to walk past him. She lost her footing and stumbled into the table. An empty wineglass fell from the counter and shattered on the floor. It wasn't merely their collision—the ground was shaking.

"Earthquake," Knox had said. He took Margot's hand. "Come here."

He'd guided her under the table and shielded her with his body from shards of glass. "Stay calm." At first, she'd tried to count the elapsing seconds, but she couldn't concentrate on anything but the incessant tremor—vibrations in the walls—and then stillness. Knox held his hand to the side of her face.

"It's okay," he said. Lane howled on the balcony, his bellows set off by traffic horns in the street below. Margot heard glass doors sliding open, neighbors' voices calling to each other from other balconies. All this time in California and not once had she experienced an earthquake so strong. Hands shaking, she couldn't believe the building hadn't collapsed on them.

She put a hand to her belly.

"You protected me," she said.

"I'm your husband. It's my job."

His eyes locked on her, and she understood that her survival was more important to him than his own. How inconsequential their argument had been. How good a father, she realized, this man would make.

"Well, someone's due for a bonus." She'd felt a rush of adrenaline and leaned in to kiss him, open-mouthed. As she guided him to their bedroom, shards of glass crackled under their feet.

Curled into Knox's arms, Margot embraced the darkness and the stillness. She wondered how the power outage could be a reaction to the earthquake nearly thirty minutes after it had occurred. Her eyes not yet adjusted, she could barely make out the photo on the bedside table of them at the chapel from when they had eloped. She squinted as she scanned the rest of their bedroom, but the relics collected over their first year of marriage—the tapestry he'd bought her from the Melrose Trading Post, the vintage vanity he'd salvaged and repurposed for her—were unfamiliar without the light.

She turned to him and said, "I'm sorry. A thousand times. I'm sorry. You know I love you. Deeper than oceans."

He lulled. "Faster than rivers."

"Stronger than waterfalls."

The power had been out for several minutes when she put her ear to his chest and listened to his heart. Beside their bed, the window let in a cool breeze. The curtains danced. Margot counted five of Knox's heartbeats before the gradual clashing of car horns, colliding metal, and shouts of rage awoke Lane in the hallway. His barking was enough to draw Knox out of bed.

"Stay here," he said. He went to the window and looked outside.

"What's going on?" Margot reached for a glass of water on the nightstand. She only saw darkness where the alarm clock's digits usually glowed red.

"Almost pitch-black," Knox said. "Everything's out but headlights."

When he came back to bed Margot huddled next to him, his warmth its own fabric in the chilled air. Lane's claws scratched the bedroom door.

"What do we do?" Margot asked. She listened closely. Eerie, she thought. So much quiet in a city so loud. "Who can we call?"

"Let's find our phones."

"We don't even have candles."

"Don't worry." He inched closer to her and kissed her cheek. "Please. Help me look for your phone."

She smiled, recognizing his genuine attempt to keep things leveled between them. "I think I saw yours in the living room," she said, "before the quake."

"Do you want to look for the phone or the flashlight?"

"I'll look for the phone."

"Then I'll look for the flashlight." He leaned over to kiss her lips. She squeezed his hand and followed him out of the bedroom. "And put your shoes on. Broken glass."

"Right," she said. Lane shot up and shoved his head into Margot's ankles.

Knox laughed. "Hasn't shown me love like that in weeks."

Lane looked up and whimpered. Margot reached down and scratched the dog's chin. "He's growing on me," she said.

Margot put on her slippers and went into the living room, Knox into the pantry. Lane whined in the bedroom. Down on the floor, Margot found her phone beneath the couch. She picked it up and clicked the home button. The screen remained black.

A white beam coming from Knox's direction illuminated the floor.

"Is it broken?" Knox asked.

"It doesn't look damaged," she said. "And it was fully charged earlier."

"Let me see." He clicked the buttons in every different way. Margot took the flashlight and pointed it around the apartment. In the darkness, all their things, like the objects in the bedroom, looked as though they belonged in someone else's life. "It's either broken or dead," Knox said. "Too bad we don't have an external charger. All we can do is plug it in. Wait until morning."

"How do we know if the Internet works?" Margot asked. "What time is it, anyway?"

He wrapped his arms around her. "It's been a long night. Let's try to get some sleep."

They returned to bed and cuddled. Lane jumped up and nestled between them, snoring within moments. Margot rubbed her feet against Knox's. Indulging in their minimal friction, she noticed a sleepy delay in his breathing. He would be passed out for the rest of the night. She lay awake, trying to hear conversations outside. Her eyes adjusted to the dark. Her thoughts circled the argument just before the earthquake: If you make that decision, I'm not sure I could handle it. Now she didn't know where she stood on the matter. All she could think about was the baby growing inside her. If her phone worked, she would have gone quietly into the other room and called her mother in Florida. They hadn't spoken much in the last year. There was no one she could talk to, not even God. How could she pray for answers? God had already deemed her unfit to be a mother. Suspended in the darkness of the bedroom, Margot lay waiting for morning.

2

Knox was first to wake. He slipped out from under Margot and checked the window. Crowds in the street were moving south toward Sunset. Margot snored, her head nuzzled into her pillow. Lane was now passed out on the floor at her bedside. The alarm clock still lacked its red blinking lights. He went to the charger and checked Margot's cell. He mashed all the buttons. No signal.

One of Margot's paintings—a turtle with the universe on its shell—hung over the breaker box. He went to it, lifted the canvas, and opened the metal circuit breaker hatch underneath. All of the breakers were still in the ON position. He flipped them from one side to the other. He walked through the apartment and checked every light switch. Still no electricity. He tested all the battery-powered devices. They worked, even Margot's old boom box. He turned its dial to the radio. Static on every station. Through the bedroom window, he could see a few small groups of people forming. Some of them looked uneasy, flailing their arms in anger. He wanted to go outside and talk to someone.

Knox thought it better to let Margot and Lane sleep. He stepped over the dog, gathered his clothes from the floor, and got dressed. He picked up one of Margot's charcoal drawing pencils and wrote in her sketchbook, 'Be Back Soon.

–K.' On the way out he placed it upright on her easel before sweeping up all the shards of glass from the floor.

By the front door hung a pink container of pepper spray. Knox had never carried weapons himself but insisted that Margot keep mace on her. Hollywood could be a dangerous place. He thought about the people outside, how hostile they looked. He tucked the pepper spray in his pocket, just in case.

When Knox reached the lobby door, he nudged it open and covered his eyes. The light was blinding after so much darkness. The intersection thrummed with chaos: Horns and revved engines. Speeding vehicles. People yelling over each other. The beep of a megaphone followed by a voice repeating the words 'Please calm down.'

Everyone had already crowded at Sunset and Vine: costumed characters, tourists, locals. He needed answers. Clearly, The Libra wasn't the only building without power. He remembered how last year the winds in Glendale had felled trees into homes. Thousands were without power for twelve hours.

At the intersection, when Knox saw the LAPD officer with a megaphone in one hand, the other hand cradling a holstered gun, he wished he'd brought his video camera. He would have gone back for it if not for Margot, if protecting her—his family—wasn't his top priority. Behind the officer, Knox saw a row of cops wielding polycarbonate shields. "Rolling blackouts are common in this city," the officer assured. "We believe last night's four-point-seven earthquake is responsible. We cannot tell you the exact details at this time, but we need everyone to return to their homes."

Knox kept walking toward the crowd. He wondered how a magnitude of less than five could strip such a big area of power.

If his phone had service, he might have used it to verify that the Northridge earthquake in '94 was upwards of a magnitude six. He looked around, tried to spot any collapsed buildings or overpasses. He smelled for a broken gas line or smoke.

"Are we in danger?" he asked nobody in particular.

The woman nearest him mumbled something in Spanish under her breath.

"Excuse me, miss," Knox held up his hand to his ear, miming a telephone. "Can I borrow your cell phone? Su teléfono?"

She eyed him up and down. "Lo siento," she said. She shook her head and walked away. Knox asked several passersby: "Should we be worried, are we safe in our homes?" but most people seemed just as lost as he was.

The officer on the megaphone repeated different variations of his earlier statement. As the original crowd dispersed, new people came to take their place. Nobody listened to the officer's commands. Knox remembered learning about the Rodney King riots of '92 in South Central, when people succumbed to assault, arson, and worse. Years ago, before moving to Los Angeles, he'd seen video footage online of fire trucks trying to extinguish block-wide blazes. The smoke appeared volcanic from the news helicopter's vantage point. His father, who had been researching LA with him, asked if he was sure about moving to a city capable of such violence.

Knox wanted to get back to Margot as soon as possible. He started for The Libra and, over the cacophony of voices, heard the officer on the megaphone shouting: "Please return to your homes. Rolling blackouts are common in Los Angeles. There is nothing to worry about."

❧

When Knox returned to The Libra, he heard mariachi music. It came from an open apartment on the way to the stairwell. He wanted to greet the musicians and ask to use one of their phones, but he had built a reputation around the building. Over the past year, most of the neighbors had heard him screaming. Knox was surprised the landlord had not evicted him. He tried everything after Tiffany: pills, therapy, total immersion in work. Nothing kept the pain from surging through him. He had found her hanging in the walk-in closet, freed her limp body from the rope, laid her on the floor. The rope had bruised her neck. Her hair spread in blonde waves, blue eyes half-open. He tried to resuscitate her. With his lips to her cold mouth, he prayed she wasn't dead. Thirty chest compressions. Two rescue breaths. Nothing brought her back.

With his head down, Knox walked past the apartment. The people inside played guitar and sang with urgency. The sound reverberated through the halls, following Knox to his apartment door. Inside he smelled cigarette smoke coming from the balcony. He went to the screen door and watched Margot paint. Lane slouched off the balcony loveseat and scampered to the screen, yawning. It was time for someone to fill his bowl.

"Hi," he said, choosing to ignore the cigarette. "Sorry about the note. I didn't want to wake you."

"It's fine," she said. "Any word of when the power will be back?"

"There was an officer with a megaphone. He just told everyone to go back to their homes. The other officers had shields like they were expecting a riot."

"I know you can take care of yourself, but please. Do not leave the apartment without me again. People in this city are nuts. This is why I wanted us to move after we got married."

I'm the one who has to protect you, Knox thought. I can't lose you too.

I won't.

"I know," he said. He opened the door for Lane. "You're right. Maybe we should have moved. But I needed to see what was going on out there. And I didn't want to risk putting you in danger."

She put her brush down on the easel and turned to him. "What do you mean?"

"I mean," he said, looking at her stomach.

"You think being pregnant makes me defenseless?"

He swallowed hard, careful of his next words. "I just want to be a good husband."

Lane yowled in the kitchen. Margot came closer to Knox. "You are," she said. "I'm sorry. I don't want to fight. I'm just a little on edge."

"I understand," he said. "I didn't mean to undermine you."

"Forget I said anything." She kissed him and went to the kitchen to fill Lane's bowl. "So how serious do you think this is?"

"Could last a couple of days," he said. "Maybe longer. It didn't look good out there. Not like a standard outage."

"I've been through hurricanes," she said. "Floods. All kinds of disasters. We can handle this."

"We should take inventory of our supplies," he said.

"Is that necessary? We have canned food and stuff."

He walked past her to the pantry. "Can you humor me and make a list with me?"

He saw her roll her eyes as she reached for a pencil and scrap of paper.

"Two cans of black beans," Knox started. "One can of chicken noodle soup. One can of minestrone. One can of vegetarian chili. Half a bag of jasmine rice. Half a loaf of sourdough bread. One pack of corn tortillas. One sleeve of gluten-free lemon wafers. A handful of trail mix. Three yellow bananas. Two tomatoes. A nearly full bag of dog food." He opened the fridge and looked inside, plugging his nose. "Last week's broiled chicken breast. A pitcher of water. Seven bottles of water. An assortment of condiments. That looks like all of our consumables." Next, he went through the bathroom cupboards for medical supplies, including a mostly useless first aid kit, a bottle of peroxide, a bottle of alcohol, aloe vera gel, suntan lotion, and four Band-Aids. Lastly, Knox wanted to cover their valuables—two dead phones, two flashlights, a can of pepper spray, a hiking pack, a small tent, kitchenware, matches, lighters, an empty gas can, paint, canvases, brushes, a video camera, lenses, SD cards, and Margot's last pack of cigarettes, which Knox argued was a valuable currency.

"There is nothing in this world that will convince me to sell those cigarettes," Margot said.

"Do you think that is the healthiest decision right now?" He tried to refrain from using the word 'pregnant.'

"I think a few cigarettes won't hurt."

He bit his lip. He'd have doused them with water if he didn't think he could pawn them, push come to shove, for a bit of food.

At their feet, Lane's chewing filled the silence.

"Well," Knox said. "I'd say we're good for at least a couple of days. Do you want to paint? You can finally teach me if you want."

Her eyes lit up. "I think I have some acrylics in the closet."

The closet. The permeation of death. Knox almost choked on his saliva. Lane barked from the doorway, swaying his snout toward his leash.

"What are we going to do about him?" Knox asked. "Why don't you gather the paints, and I'll take him for a quick walk?"

Margot stared at him askance. The dog huffed.

"Ten minutes?" she said.

"Ten minutes."

Lane's tail thumped against the door. Knox latched the leash to the dog's collar and blew Margot a kiss. She caught it midair, held it to her chest. On the way outside, Knox passed the mariachi-playing neighbors again. This time he stopped at their doorway and knocked.

"Hi there," he said. "Sorry to bother you. If it isn't too much trouble, could I use your phone?"

"No service," one of them said in broken English. "Must be a tower down."

"Thanks, anyway."

They carried on with their music as if they didn't have a care in the world. How enviable, Knox thought. He followed Lane outside. While the dog did its business, Knox kept a distance from passersby—superheroes, cyclists, homeless people yelling obscenities. He could hear sirens and shouting, engines and screeching brakes.

Dear K.,

We've been making progress in strides at the lab. I know I've been working so much that I may as well live here. But our developments have been so exciting I feel I'm making a difference. I feel, for once, like my work matters.

Like it could change the world.

To this, I say:

I'm sorry for being absent. Distant. I've decided to start writing you letters because only so much can be said through a text message. I'd call you, but I have a feeling you're asleep right now.

The exciting news is that the particle accelerator is almost finished.

Dr. Tajū believes it's a mere matter of weeks before we'll be ready to begin the first tests. The way he's described it, our particle accelerator will make the

Large Hadron Collider seem like two-way radio compared to the Internet.[∞]

Nerdy, I know.

But that's why you love me.

I must get back to work now. Dr. Tajū needs me to hop on the supercomputer to run a few simulations. My goal? Illustrate what happens when two particles collide at the speed of light.

Piece of cake.

Oh, before I forget!

I've attached a photo of us last year at Death Valley.

Do you remember how the wildflowers were in super bloom? Apparently, there had been a downpour in the fall, strong enough to induce flash floods. A rare occurrence for the desert. The storm revealed dormant seeds in the ground, which helped them sprout. And they super bloomed!

[∞] Without the Large Hadron Collider, our collider would not be possible. The LHC lay the groundwork for the next generation of particle colliders, this is true; however, the LHC still failed in many areas of its projected successes. Ex: Matter could never have been compressed to the required density with only eight toroidal magnets. Our collider has twenty-nine.

It was a once-in-a-decade event, and we had no idea.

Lucky us.

For us, it was Life Valley for a day.

Give Lane a kiss for me.[∞]

Love,
T.

[∞] I miss our boy! I ordered a new chew toy to be sent to the apartment. I couldn't resist. I just want to spoil him! I love our little family. I swear that working so much will prove worth it.

THE WALK-IN CLOSET was filled with all of Margot's studio materials: Early drawings and paintings. Cans of varnish and paint thinner. Supplies she had accumulated over the five years she'd been in Los Angeles. Most of the paintings were of Venice Beach, back when she would sit on the shore-adjacent deck for hours, painting and listening to Janis Joplin. LA was so new then. She had her whole life in front of her. But more than Margot's art supplies filled the closet—she couldn't ignore that bitter air of death. There was nowhere else to store anything in their small apartment except for the very space where Tiffany had taken her life. It was enough to make Margot hold her breath whenever she had to enter.

The acrylics were on the topmost shelf. Margot had climbed up her ladder to reach for a jar of gesso when the blood rushed to her face, and she grew suddenly dizzy. She put her hand against the wall to keep her balance, but her eyes went blurry and she lost her footing.

"You slept for eight hours," Knox said. Margot felt the damp rag on her forehead. "In a few minutes, I want you to drink some water. And we should get some food in you. Your body needs protein."

What had made her pass out? Dehydration? Hunger? Shock? Her hands went to her stomach. "What if—"

"Don't worry," Knox said. He cradled her hands, his fingers warm on her belly. "You're fine. Everything's fine."

"How do you know?"

"I just know."

She tried to rise despite his nurturing hold on her. No good—movement only fueled more dizziness.

"What time is it?" she asked.

"Eleven is my guess."

"AM or PM?"

"PM."

"What about Lane? When was the last time he was out?"

"You fell while I was taking him for a walk. He's been good, and I haven't left your side since."

Margot lay there for a minute, eyes adjusting to the darkness, trying to forget the probing sensation of Tiffany's spirit. It felt like condensation on her skin, making the hairs rise on the back of her neck. Don't be stupid, Margot thought. There's no such thing as spirits.

"So, what do you want first?" Knox said. "The good news or the bad?"

She squinted at him. "Good?"

"I can make you delicious black bean tacos."

"Bad?"

"The beans are going to be room temperature."

She stuck out her tongue.

"It's not the end of the world," he joked.

"Don't jinx us."

Knox handed her a bottle of water. She took several gulps, and water trickled down the sides of her face.

"Easy," Knox said. "Relax for a bit. I'll prepare the tacos."

Lane ran into the bedroom when Knox opened the door. "Someone missed you," he said. The dog jumped into the bed and licked her fingers. He whinnied, looking at her with pouty eyes.

"Damn dog." She petted him until Knox came back, holding the plates with a waiter's finesse.

"Two Blackout Tacos for the lady," he said. He told Lane to go into the other room and sat next to Margot. On the plates were little piles of beans spooned into corn tortillas. Knox had even diced tomatoes and sprinkled them on top.

"You're sweet," she said. Knox took the first bite as if to prove their edibility. Margot sat up straight, picked up one of the lukewarm tacos, and put it in her mouth. It tasted good once she got over the dry texture. They sat in silence, eating until every bite was gone. She exhaled, feeling strong for the first time since she woke.

"I was worried about you," Knox said. "No way to call 911."

"Right," she said. What the hell would she have done in his shoes? She hated how helpless she felt, so wan in such a critical circumstance. "Thank you. For taking care of me. I don't know what happened."

"You're okay," he said, reaching for her stomach. "That's all that matters."

"I have to go to a doctor as soon as the power is back."

Knox retracted his hand. "I agree. As soon as the power is back."

❧

The next morning Margot felt stir-crazy. She hadn't been outside since the quake. When they took Lane out for the bathroom, she saw the crowds at Hollywood and Vine, armed officers with their megaphones and shields, droves of people trying to get information. They were standing in front of The Libra when Knox told her the crowd had doubled in size since the day before.

"What about the radio?" Margot said. "Shouldn't there be updates? Someone has to know how much of LA has gone dark."

"I don't think the normal radio is working," he said. "That's why everyone's out here looking for answers. Most people are used to relying on their phones."

Before going back inside, Knox checked the Jeep. The building's parking was not gated, which, according to Knox, meant that anyone from the street could meander in, shatter the windows, leave them without a car.

"But we have a boot on the tire," she said. "And a club on the steering wheel. I don't think it's going anywhere."

"I was considering siphoning the gas," he said. "I'm worried about someone stealing it. If gas stations don't have power, nobody can purchase fuel."

"Are you sure that's something we have to worry about?" She couldn't imagine people so desperate for gasoline they'd siphon it through a hose. Then again, she'd always had the luxury of stopping at a station when low or calling roadside assistance when she ran out.

"Did you see the crowds out there? I don't want to be stranded here if it comes to that."

He had a point. She didn't want to be stranded, either. She looked to the sky, past The Libra and its neighboring buildings. There were no clouds and, Margot realized, no aircraft.

"Have you seen any planes?" she asked. "Helicopters?"

"No, but that's a good observation."

"Are we going to run out of supplies?"

"Not sure. But I can only assume it's just a matter of time before there's a riot. Or looting. Or worse."

Margot wondered what would happen with the baby. If she could get to a clinic, there was still time to start the hormone-blocking medication. She'd learned, before the pregnancy test validated her suspicions, that the medication was the simplest way to go about early termination. If only Knox had taken her side during the argument, if only he'd supported her decision to be rid of it, Margot would have felt more comfortable discussing with him what was best for her and her body. On the way back upstairs Margot said, "I wish we had family here. Or at least friends to talk to."

"Yesterday I asked the people downstairs to use their phone," Knox said. "They said there was no service, that a tower must be down."

"But how sure can we be? How do we know they just don't have bad service?"

"What do you suggest? Going door-to-door asking to use people's phones?"

Knox closed the door behind them. Margot sat on the couch. "Maybe. If that's what it takes. You tell me. What would a good husband do in this situation?"

He let out a sardonic laugh.

"You're using my words against me." He shook his head, went to the balcony, and lit a cigarette.

Why was she on the offense? Because he was in favor of keeping the child?

"I'm not trying to take it out on you," she offered. "I'm just starting to get worried."

"You don't think I feel bad that we don't have any friends?" Knox said. "You're not the only one who lost connections after we got married, you know."

Margot watched him exhale, the plume of smoke drifting past her canvas. He wasn't typically one to get defensive. But after the last year of living together, she'd noticed her worrying could take a toll on him. She'd tried to get better, but she couldn't control the unwanted thoughts. The fear.

"I'm not trying to make you feel guilty," she said. Knox exhaled again and put out the cigarette. She sat next to him. "If the shit were to hit the fan, I'd be useless without you."

Knox sat up.

"You'd be fine without me." He put his finger under her chin and pressed upward until their eyes met. "Take a deep breath." She did. "Now let it out." She did. A fraction of the worry melted away.

"We'll give it another day," he said. "If the power isn't back tomorrow, we'll get in the car. We'll try to find a phone, a doctor."

"Is it just me or does it feel silly?"

"Does what feel silly?"

"How reliant we are. On technology. Phones. The Internet. I keep wanting to check my email. Ask Google about miscarriage rates. It's probably better this way."

Knox furled his eyebrows. "You're not going to miscarry."

She bit her lip. "Don't say that."

"What am I supposed to say?"

"I need to talk to someone."

"You can talk to me."

"Someone else." Again, she'd spoken too soon.

Knox hung his head. "I just want to take care of you, Margot. I love you."

She couldn't hold back the tears. She left the balcony and went straight to the bathroom. She closed the door, sat on the toilet, and wept into her hands. Memories flashed through her mind: The D & C. The emptiness. The doctor numbing her cervix, removing the lining of her uterus. She forced the thoughts from her mind until there was only breathing. She felt the cold linoleum floor against her bare feet.

Funny how she'd do anything—lock herself in a bathroom, leave Venice, have an affair, hide a pregnancy test—to avoid confronting the things in life that brought her pain.

"Baby," Knox said from the other side of the door. "Everything is okay. Just let me know you're okay."

"I'm okay," she said. "I just need a minute."

She didn't know which was worse, the dark corners of her thoughts or the real world. In her thoughts, ghosts could haunt her. In the real world, things could die. When she'd lost the baby, she couldn't have imagined the effect it would have on Jason.

Could she do the same thing to Knox?

To herself?

"I'm here if you need me," Knox said.

Margot kept her mouth shut. Inflicting pain on Knox was now inevitable, no matter her decision. Or God's. She curled into a ball on the floor. Funny, she thought. How powerless we've been all this time.

4

Knox wasn't about to pick a fight. He preferred to sit on the balcony with the dog, listening to Hollywood's rapid heartbeat. He'd be there for Margot when she was ready to talk. If only they could talk about the matter without the added pressure of the blackout, maybe then he would understand her position. Before they married, he'd assumed that husbands and wives talked about everything.

Now he knew the truth of it.

For example, he couldn't tell Margot that sometimes, when he was alone with Lane, he thought about Tiffany. So smart, Tiffany. One of the brightest people Knox had ever met. Six years they had been together. It felt like forever since he first saw her at a lame house party playing beer pong with the rest of the physics majors. Tiffany's face had been stern, aiming the Ping-Pong ball like a homing missile. Later, he'd introduced himself when they were waiting for the keg with a pickup line he'd lifted from *Before Sunrise*.

"I love that movie," she'd said. "I've seen your documentaries at the on-campus screenings. I like that you ask serious questions about life and existence. That's why I study astrophysics. I want all the answers."

It had been Tiffany's endless curiosity that most attracted Knox. They could discuss the work of both Stephen

Hawking and Richard Linklater. Tiffany often spent hours talking about her thesis: Galileon theory. Wormholes. The secrets of quantum space-time. Some of her research was over his head, but he'd still found her mind fascinating. If it wasn't astrophysics she was talking about, it was her other obsession—mythology. She'd often recited Virgil and Ovid and explained to Knox the variations of the story of Orpheus and Eurydice throughout antiquity. "Would you come for me?" she'd once asked him during a day trip to Lake Erie. They had stood side-by-side, casting stones into the calm waters. The chill of the autumn air brought their bodies close; they were but moments from their first kiss. "Would you descend into the mouth of the underworld to get me back?" She'd smiled devilishly and ensnared him in her arms. He watched the ripples fan out over the surface of the lake and told her that he'd sacrifice it all. He told her even hell couldn't keep him away, and he leaned in to press his lips to hers.

They were both Toledoans, yet their paths had never crossed, and Knox had known enough to not let her go: sweet, shy, sexy in her disheveled hair and bent glasses kind of way. He couldn't have done better than her in that city, even his father had told him so. The first four years had flown by: college, intimacy, monogamy, getting to know each other's families. The memories were often enough to send Knox into a depression. After graduation, Tiffany was offered a lofty position researching quantum physics at UCLA. Moving across the country together had felt like the right thing to do. Of course, their families had questioned whether they had plans for marriage—they had, after all, already invested four years into the relationship—but he and Tiffany had simply laughed it off, said, "Maybe someday."

It wasn't like he hadn't thought of proposing, but the move to LA had been tougher than they'd anticipated. A higher cost of living meant Tiffany working overtime in the lab while Knox waited tables between production gigs. What little time they'd had together consisted mostly of talking about work, having sex, or the occasional stroll around one of their favorite parts of LA. Although the nature of Tiffany's job had been classified—a project funded by private international sources—she'd often hinted around at her work with the esteem of a revolutionary.

"It's pretty simple," she'd explained one night post-coitus. "When you're able to manipulate matter on an atomic or subatomic level, a rift is possible. The only problem, then, is what's on the other side." When Knox had told her he couldn't picture it, she drew a sketch—a snake in a circle. "The ouroboros. It eats its tail. Never-ending. No beginning, no end. It just exists. Matter works the same way. And time. You eliminate the possibility of future or past."

Tiffany was the reason he'd become obsessed with documenting anomalies. "If I had to guess," she'd once said while discussing his filmography over lunch at their favorite beachside restaurant in Venice, "I would categorize your interests as paradoxical. You're fascinated by mysteries. The unknown. The outliers in life that cannot be explained. Which is probably why you love me so much." She'd laughed at her joke, their love as evident and unquestionable as the earth beneath them.

But for every ounce of Tiffany's intelligence was an equal amount of narcissism.

He'd been a fool to think, even for a moment, that it was about him.

Her last act.

The ultimate passive-aggressive move.

He clenched his jaw, shifted his attention to The Libra's balcony aglow in the twilight. He drew a line through the ashes piled in the tray beside him. Lane crawled up to the loveseat and put his chin on Knox's leg. Knox wondered if the dog could have possibly been thinking about Tiffany too. It had been six months after moving to LA when Tiffany brought up the idea of getting a dog. She'd said, "Let's see if we can handle raising something together." Knox never questioned it. They'd gone to the nearest animal shelter and fell in love with the first dog they saw, a little Golden Labrador.

"Just came in today," the vet tech had said. "Probably be gone tomorrow. You're the first family to see him."

The first family. Knox knew that had been the phrase that sold Tiffany. That night they'd played with the puppy for hours, trained it to sit and roll, to not pee on the carpet. Tiffany had been so adamant about Lane being a well-behaved dog.

"That name," Knox said. "Where'd you come up with it? Is it supposed to be like the lane in a street? A bowling alley?"

Tiffany smiled. "After the particle physicist Kenneth Lane. He was known for supercollider physics and changing the face of hadron physics. He is a major influence on my work. Especially RIFT."

"Your side project," he'd said. "Something about quantum fields. Breaking spontaneous symmetry."

"Close enough," she laughed.

"Lane." Knox picked up the puppy and held it like an infant. "I like it."

"It's official," Tiffany said. "We're a family."

Knox had felt like nothing could ever go wrong. They'd keep working, watch the dog get bigger, move into a house one day.

Or so he'd hoped.

He never would have imagined betraying her.

Lane had passed out before the darkness fell, and Knox hadn't heard a word from Margot. He figured she was still in the bathroom, possibly sleeping in the tub. He lit a cigarette, the last in the pack. Good riddance, he thought. He'd taken up intermittent smoking right after their first therapy session. It didn't matter how much they talked about Tiffany—nothing erased the guilt. And there had been the note the therapist told them to destroy. The note Margot had burned. The note Knox couldn't get out of his memory.

Do you believe in life after death?

The sounds from the street had vanquished, if only briefly. No helicopters. No cars. No megaphones. No shouting. Only Lane's soft snoring. Knox took a long, hard drag on the cigarette, and he gently shut his eyes.

Knox awoke to someone pounding on the door. The cigarette had burned a hole in the loveseat's armrest. Was Margot still in the bathroom? A new day's sunlight beamed onto the balcony. Who could have been knocking on the door so early?

There it was again. A rapid pounding. Three thuds. Knox slid the screen door open and went into the living room.

"Margot?" he whispered.

Three more thuds. "Open the door," a voice bellowed. Deep. Male. Confident. Knox crept to the front door.

"Hi," Knox said, quiet. Firm. "How can I help you?"

"Open the door," the voice said. Knox looked through the peephole. Five men. Were they in uniform? He couldn't tell with the hallway so dark.

"Who are you?"

"FBI."

What the hell were the Feds doing outside his door? Knox remembered The Libra's lack of gated entry. He thought it possible they weren't who they said they were. He pressed his hands together and held them to his lips. That's when he saw the pink canister of mace hanging in front of him.

"What cause do you have to be at my residence, sir?"

"We don't need cause, sir," the voice echoed. "Open the door."

Knox looked around for Lane, who must have still been asleep on the balcony. What good was having a dog if not to fend off potential intruders?

"With all due respect," Knox said, "why would I open my door to strangers? Can you show me some identification?"

"We're conducting a time-sensitive investigation," the voice said. "We're going to need you to open this door now."

He heard Margot's footsteps behind him.

"What's going on?" she asked, groggily. "Is everything okay?"

He turned from the door to look at her and brought his voice to a whisper. "I think so. There are half a dozen guys on the other side. They say they're the FBI."

"Open it," she said. "The last thing we need is for you to get arrested because you failed to comply." Her eyes were wide, hair trussed.

"Look," Knox said, "what if they're not the FBI? For all I know they could come in here, kill me, or worse."

"Isn't that a little extreme?" she said.

Three more thuds at the door.

"I think you're underestimating what people are capable of."

He motioned for her to sit. "I'm serious," the voice said. "If you don't open up, we will have no choice but to use force."

"Alright," Knox said. He opened the door, lock by lock.

The man who'd been speaking stood in front of four others. They all wore black shirts, pants, and baseball caps. Knox looked for badges but saw none.

The man on Knox's far left held up a piece of paper with a sketch on it; he and the officer next to him compared Knox's face, eyeing him up and down. The man on Knox's right flashed a light onto Margot, and another shone one into Knox's face.

"Just you and your wife in here?" Unable to see them, Knox shielded his eyes from the beam. He felt in his gut the flutter of vulnerability. He kept his mind on the mace, prepared to use it in an instant.

"Just me and my wife," he said. "Is there something wrong?"

"Are you aiding and abetting a criminal?"

"No, sir. We're not."

The man looked back to the others and shook his head. The man holding the sketch folded it, put it in his pocket. The two wielding flashlights turned them off.

"Who are you looking for?" Knox asked. "Are we in danger? Do you know anything about when the power will be back on?"

Four of the men walked away. The remaining man, the one who had been speaking, stopped and said, "I'm sorry. We're looking for a potential criminal in the area. Didn't mean to alarm. You and your wife have a wonderful day." He smiled and followed the others into the shadows.

"Close the door," Margot said. "Please."

He did and bolted all the locks. He turned around, looked at his wife, and opened his mouth. What did he expect to do with a canister of mace? He didn't stand a chance against them. It felt like a miracle that they were safe again, yet he couldn't speak for fear of sobbing. He wanted to say, 'They could have hurt you.' He looked into her eyes. He didn't need to say anything. They were not safe anymore. Could he protect himself and his wife from a group of men? No. Not without a gun.

"I need to sit down," he said. She brought him to the couch and put her head against his shoulder. Lane staggered in from the balcony.

"Do you think their so-called investigation is real?" Margot said. "I can't decide if they were telling the truth. How are we supposed to know what to believe?"

He scratched behind Lane's ears, images of what they could have done to Margot running through his head. "I don't know," he said. "But we're not going to sit around while they plan to break in."

Later that day, Knox dug out his old hiking pack, sleeping bag, and tent from the closet. He'd held his breath and fought back the memories of Tiffany. If he wanted to keep Margot safe, he needed to forget the past. Not erase it—Lord knew how many times he'd proffered that advice to Margot. Simply forget the past—for now—and protect his wife, and child, at all costs.

He sorted through the old pack on the balcony. It was empty except for a few bungee cords, carabiners, and a map of LA. How would he get them out of the city? What was the nearest place with power?

Margot had spent the morning working on a new landscape, one she must have started in her old apartment. She'd set up the new canvas beside the one of Hollywood on which she'd been working before the quake. Knox recognized the view of Venice Beach from when he'd frequented the boardwalk with Tiffany. In Margot's painting, the ocean was on the right, the boardwalk on the left. The shoreline divided both sides evenly, which Knox thought a harmonic balance of nature and industrialization. She'd rigged her old battery-powered boom box and painted while listening to Janis Joplin's "One Good Man" on repeat for hours. He couldn't help but wonder if she'd been thinking about Jason.

Lane came outside, sniffed the contents of Knox's pack, and gnawed on a bone.

"Those men could have overpowered me," Knox said. "We have to face reality. We don't know what could happen. We have more than ourselves to think about now."

Margot's gaze remained fixed on her new painting. "And there aren't men out there who can overpower you?" She exhaled. "The truth is that we need to accept how powerless we are."

"We're not powerless," Knox said. "Last year in Tallahassee hundreds of thousands went without power for a week after the hurricane."

"That was a hurricane," Margot said. "This is different."

"Scranton, Pennsylvania," Knox said. "Hundreds of thousands without power due to a windstorm. In Kenya, there was a blackout because of a monkey in a power station. Anything can happen."

"You know a lot about power outages."

Of course he did. Tiffany had practically been a human encyclopedia on the subject. "We have to be tactical," he said, changing the topic. "We have to think twice about everything we do. How we use our resources."

"So, you're willing to become homeless to find answers?"

"If you don't want to go, we don't have to. But, eventually, we're going to run out of food and water, assuming those guys don't come back first."

"What if we leave and they come back?" Margot said. "What if they kick the door in?"

"You're not listening to me," he said. "You were right. We should have left LA when we got married. I want to put this place behind me. What better time to start over than now? What if we pack the Jeep, and then we just leave? We don't have to come back."

"What are we going to do?" Margot said. "Leave a note for the landlord?"

He told her they'd call him when they found a phone, that the biggest threat was staying in The Libra without the proper means to protect themselves.

"If it's up to me," Knox said, "we'll be somewhere with power before sunset. I think we should try to pack up the car as soon as possible." He unfolded the map of LA on the balcony floor and invited her to sit with him. He wanted to give her a visual, put her on the same page as him. "Our best bet is to travel east. I want to avoid going north. If we get on the 405 there'll be nothing but gridlock traffic. My goal would be to get past Glendale and try our luck there. Don't you want to call our families and let them know we're okay? If we can fill up on gas there, we'll keep going."

"And what if we can't? We don't know anybody in Glendale."

He thought about all the friends that stopped talking to him after Tiffany. Margot's friends, too, had distanced themselves when they found out her fling with Knox led to Tiffany's suicide.

"We don't have anyone here anymore, period."

He watched Margot tear at a corner of the map, refusing to look at him. "There's one person," she said.

Knox chewed the inside of his cheek. "I don't count him."

"And why not?"

"Because he's your ex." He caught his voice before it got too loud.

"He might have power. He would let us stay in his house."

Knox wanted to tell her he didn't care whether the guy lived or died.

"That's the last thing I would do," he said.

"What about me?" Margot said. "I have to be here every day, in the building where you lived with her."

"Okay," he said. He couldn't stomach thinking about Tiffany. "You have a point, but I don't think it's a good idea to go west. We should go inland."

"Why? What difference is it going to make?"

"If we go to Venice and something happens then we're barricaded. You don't want to be trapped with the ocean at your back. We only have so much gas. There's no telling when we can get more."

"I'm starting to think you're making this out to be worse than it is."

He wanted to bring up the Rodney King riots, but he didn't want to alarm her any more than necessary. He just wanted her to trust him.

"Well," he said, "I'm starting to think you're not taking it seriously enough."

He watched her purse her lips as she went inside. "Let's go, boy," he heard her say to the dog. "Time for a walk. We need some fresh air."

Knox remained on the balcony while Margot put the leash on Lane and left the apartment. He would give her space even though his gut told him not to let her go without him, that he should be the bigger person and swallow his pride. She'll only be in front of the building, he thought. She has the dog with her. No need to worry.

He focused on the map beneath his fingers, visualizing a route that avoided Little Armenia and Koreatown. They would search for power. They would find a way to contact their families. They would have absolutely no reason at all to resort to Jason.

Dear K.,

I would just like you to know I enjoyed myself yesterday. I'd been looking forward to a day with just you and Lane, and even though I know you planned out our whole day, you made it all feel effortless.

The Venice canals, the beach, Small World Books, riding around on scooters, a delectable lamb gyro lunch.

You know how to show a girl a good time.

But honestly. Walking the canals with you felt like a dream. A reverie. I thought, 'Here we are in Los Angeles. We worked so hard to move here, what once felt like a dream. A dream made real.'

Sometimes when we take our walks, I feel like we're in the Before Sunrise *trilogy. You're Ethan Hawke and I'm Julie Delpy, only not French. We've watched those movies so many times, I wonder if I've fixed us in their image. Walking and talking, being present and making sense of the universe.*

Speaking of the universe.

Dr. Tajū was impressed with my simulations and has decided to let me run and design the first few tests once the particle collider is complete. I had to prove that our particle accelerator wouldn't swallow the Earth.

No big deal.

But honestly, being trusted to run and design the first tests is both an honor and a large responsibility. Dr. Tajū says he's too close to the collider, that he's spent so much of his life on it he can no longer see the forest for the trees. He says he needs a pair of fresh eyes, ones he can rely upon.

Apparently, those eyes are mine.

However, I still have quite a few simulations to get through while the building of the collider is still in its final stages. For example: Can I prove that the universe is expanding, and is it possible to alter it?

Think that one's a doozy?

Try this one on for size:

Assuming that string theorists are correct, can I prove that we experience three full-sized spatial dimensions every day?[∞]

[∞] The path to infinities is paved in String Theories. To understand the extra dimensions implied by String Theory, one must envision the ten dimensions as literal strings wound up so tightly they are imperceptible in any exterior dimension. If String Theory leads us to supergravity, and supergravity must be married to quantum mechanics to spawn a black hole, then it follows: We must begin to walk the path to infinities.

I've got my work cut out for me, K.

And only a couple of weeks to do so. Of the twenty-three-mile underground ring of magnets, they still have three miles left to build. Dr. Tajū is already eyeing the Nobel, but I think he's jumping the gun.

Right about now, I'm missing snuggles with you and Lane. I know that when we moved here, we didn't realize I'd be so busy. And when we got Lane, I was so excited to finally start a family with you. Now I'm the one who's gone all the time. But then again, I never thought I'd be lucky enough to work with someone on Dr. Tajū's level of prestige. Who would have thought someone would read my thesis on supercollider physics and spontaneous symmetry? I feel I'm making a sacrifice, spending so much time here. I feel I'm missing out on the more important things in life. Our small moments. But I also feel I'm on the verge of—dare I say it?—Greatness.

And I must believe you'll forgive me.

Now that the Event Horizon Telescope collaboration captured the first-ever photograph of a black hole, Tajū is relentless. He believes it imperative to complete and release our findings before another organization, like EHT, gets there first.

I hope you're finding ways to use your talents here, too. We moved here so I could take the job at UCLA, and you've been nothing but supportive of me. Don't forget that I still believe in your vision behind the camera.[∞] *If you want to pursue making documentaries, or do something else with your life, I support you either way. It's the least I can do, considering how patient you've been with me. I don't want you to feel down because you're waiting tables—so many people must be doing that in this city to pursue their dreams. And don't worry about money. If there is one benefit to my spending so much time here, it is the salary. Remember that I've always loved your fascination with anomalies, and I know your break will come one day.*

Yours always,

T.

[∞] You know how much I loved your early work. Even the simple documentary about the leaves changing in autumn and then returning in the spring. It wasn't the subject matter you were tackling that impressed me; it was the way in which you filmed the trees, the leaves. Your artistry was evident with each angle, each lens choice. Also in the editing, which implied that time itself is an anomaly. There is a truth in the way we tell our stories which could never be conveyed by mere linearity. Sometimes parts of the story, or the facts, must be told out of order to get at the heart of a truth. I think that piece spoke to me so deeply because of its simplicity. Leaves changing color. Leaves returning, but never in the same form. The endless cycle of rebirth.

5

MARGOT SAT IN the passenger seat with the dog while Knox packed the Jeep. She couldn't believe they were about to leave The Libra. What were the chances she could convince him to go to Venice and stay with Jason?

"Why Glendale of all places?" she said. "You said it yourself: 'We have more than ourselves to think about now.' Wouldn't putting the past behind us and going to Jason's be more surefire than winging it?"

Knox started the engine. "Just pretend it's an ordinary trip," he said. "What did the therapist call that thing you do? Catastrophizing. There's no need to do that. We're going to be okay." He made it sound so simple, albeit patronizing. As if she could so easily turn off the thoughts of them driving to their deaths. A day trip, she thought. He's not listening to reason. Out of curiosity and desperate for music, she clicked on the radio.

"You probably won't find anything but static," Knox said.

She hated that he was right. Still, she tried all the buttons. Static, static, static.

"You can sing," Knox said, smiling. "I probably know all the words to 'One Good Man' by now."

"I'd rather sit in silence if you don't mind." She rolled down her window, letting in the humid air. "Is it me, or does it feel like we're in the middle of a heat wave?"

He rolled down his window and stuck out his hand. "It's possible. At this point, nothing would surprise me."

She searched the faces outside for expressions of fear, concern—a trick the therapist had taught her. "When you feel yourself catastrophizing," she'd said, "try to gauge the emotions of people around you." The therapist had even shown her a chart of little faces in rows and columns portraying dozens of emotions. "Study them," the therapist said. Margot had done so: Disgust. Fear. Worry. Hatred. Joy. Contentment. Wonder. "You can learn so much from studying the face. The way people are feeling, possibly what they're thinking." Knox hated it when Margot tried to read his face. He'd said the therapist's argument was based on an outdated study. Sometimes Margot liked to guess his emotions. More often than not she guessed correctly. She could always tell if something was bothering him, if he was hiding something. Right now, for example, while he drove, he chewed the side of his cheek. *There's something he's not telling me*, she thought. There was the option of opening her mouth, asking what was wrong, but there was also the option to keep a tight lip, pretend she didn't know. On a regular day—one where they could stop for sushi or ride the roller coaster at the Santa Monica Pier—maybe she would have addressed the issue, opened channels of communication, as the therapist had recommended. But this wasn't a regular day. She wouldn't dare add to the stockpile of problems that had already started to burn like kindling.

But if she was to have any agency in her situation, what good would simply reading her surroundings do? *Look where your analytical mind has gotten you*, she thought. *Either passenger or escape artist. Such has been my role to play.*

A role of my choosing, no less.

In the backseat, Lane turned in circles. "There, there, boy," Margot said. She reached to pat the dog's head. Moments like this, she felt like they were a family. Her, Knox, and Lane. Each of them with their dysfunctional pasts. Could the dog feel sadness? Could it understand pain? Sometimes Margot thought she could see it in his eyes, the same way she could tell when Knox was thinking of Tiffany. Perhaps he and the dog were psychically linked. What was it called—canine telepathy?

"He's fine," Knox said. "He may not look it, but that dog's got a lot of fight in him. I've seen him chase down a squirrel, or two." Lane bayed and stuck his head between theirs. "Yep, as long as we got Lane, we'll be safe. You'll take care of me and your momma, won't you, boy?" The dog yipped and licked Knox's face, then hers.

She dried her cheek and let her hair blow around in the hot wind. She mentally summoned the words 'Everything will be fine' and looked out the window to the once-familiar donut shops, plazas, and liquor stores. Now, they were all locked up or boarded. At the intersections, no traffic signals worked. Nor were there cops or traffic controllers. Everything will be fine, she thought. Lane moaned, panting with his tongue out. "It feels like torture to leave him in here," Margot said. She took out one of the several water bottles they'd brought, unscrewed the lid, and poured some into Lane's mouth. When she turned around, she thought the incoming heat more unbearable than Florida's. Still, she could close her eyes, pretend she was back home, on the beach. She could let the heat coerce her into a nap, into imagining being eighteen again, sneaking shots of tequila from an opaque bottle. She thought about her and Jason, how they used to party for hours, getting drunk and tan. They'd talked about living forever, starting a family on the West Coast. It had been Margot's dream, having Jason's baby, being a mother. She'd learned a miscarriage could destroy that dream: hopelessness, self-hatred, nightmares of being hollowed out like a tree. Was it foolish to have had unprotected sex with her husband, considering what she'd gone through? Not that it was planned with Jason; they weren't married—or engaged, for that matter—but Margot hadn't needed such placeholders. She'd loved Jason and, her eyes closed, still imagining the shores of Miami Beach, she considered that she may always care for him, in some way, even though she was certain of her future with Knox.

She then remembered meeting Knox while walking at Runyon Canyon where a part of the ground had nearly split in two. "Watch your step," he'd said. "I'd hate for you to get stuck in there." He kicked a stone into the mouth of the small crater. She'd looked down, about fifteen feet of rock.

"You may have just saved my life," she'd said. It had been four months since she'd left the apartment. The thought of meeting another man had never even crossed her mind—let alone the man who, after months of growing distant from Jason, would show her happiness was still possible, even if happiness looked like outdoor movies at the Hollywood Forever cemetery or world-famous hotdogs at Pink's. Of course, she hadn't yet known about Tiffany.

Knox wouldn't reveal that information until it was too late.

"You look like you could use a cup of coffee," Knox had said, reaching across the chasm to shake her hand. She had not planned to fall in love with him, just like she had not planned to grow to hate the thought of Jason, who had wanted to try for another baby only two weeks after she'd left the hospital. Who had bunkered down in his Venice fortress when she refused.

So much for plans, Margot thought.

When she opened her eyes, she did a double take—for a second it looked like they were at the Disneyland parking lot on a holiday. How long had she dozed off?

"Where are we?"

The Jeep was stopped. Outside, a line of police cars blocked the bridge. "They're not letting anyone cross the LA River," Knox answered.

Margot looked around, eyes still heavy from her nap. Horns blared, louder than outside The Libra after the earthquake. "What the hell are we supposed to do?" she asked. Lane growled out the window. Margot saw LAPD officers exiting their cruisers and approaching people's vehicles. One of them, a woman, walked up to Margot's side of the Jeep. Margot could see her name, Rotura, on her uniform.

"Good afternoon," the officer said. "City's on lockdown. Best be heading back home, or to a shelter, if you don't have a residence."

"Lockdown?" Margot said. She couldn't help herself. "But we need to leave the city. There must be another road or something. Please, Officer Rotura. We're just trying to go to Glendale."

"Not possible," Rotura said.

"It's okay," Knox said, reaching to touch Margot, a plea for her to be quiet.

"Wait," Margot said, ignoring his hand. "There's no radio. We have no idea what's going on. Not since the earthquake. When will there be electricity? When will things be back to normal? I just found out I'm pregnant." Margot thought that, certainly, from woman to woman, Officer Rotura would provide them with even the slightest bit of information.

But she didn't. The officer backed away, shaking her head and waving her traffic baton. Who were they to be denied answers? They were, after all, tax-paying citizens. She had half a mind to tell Knox to pull over, stop the car.

"There's nothing we can do," he insisted. "If she's saying the city is on lockdown, it must be more serious than we thought." He joined the line of vehicles forming around the block. Traffic inched forward more slowly than rush hour on the 405.

So much for plans.

"Now what?" Margot said. "We can't leave. We have nowhere to go. No way of getting in touch with anyone. There must be a usable phone or source of news somewhere in this city. Right? I mean, I'm not crazy, am I? Is it too much to want to know what the hell is going on?"

"No, it's not. I just don't know what to tell you. There was an earthquake, and now there's no power. The police won't let anyone out of the city. We have no phone, no Internet, no radio. But we're two intelligent people. We just have to put our minds together and we'll get through this."

Once they cleared the traffic jam, Knox turned down Silver Lake Boulevard. Margot saw rows of tents erected along the reservoir, people outside them communing on the grass. Compared to living out of a tent, being back at The Libra with dwindling food was a luxury. She considered how quickly the bad had grown worse, and how much worse this disaster could still get.

"Let's go home," she said. "We can't say we didn't try. We'll ration everything. Maybe we can barter with our neighbors."

"Too bad I smoked your last cigarette," Knox said. "Probably could have gotten a loaf of bread for it." He smiled and nudged her knee.

"You're unbelievable," she said, giving him a sinister grin. She loved that he wanted to lighten the mood, make things feel better than they were. Still, she wanted that cigarette.

Dear K.,

I'm waiting for some of our assistants to report back with the results from my latest simulation testing the boundaries of Langrarian vortices.

What fun photons and turbulence can be.

Speaking of turbulence.

I've been thinking about home.

When we lived in Ohio, I used to imagine a different life for us.

One with daily views of palm trees, the ocean, sunshine.

And we made that different life happen.

But I must admit, there is a surprising lack of sunshine in our lab. I'm underground all day. I see cement walls, not palm trees. I see a lovely painting of the ocean against a cement wall, not the actual ocean.

Every so often, I catch myself imagining yet another life for us.

One in which I perhaps study literature or films instead of black holes. One in which you don't feel the need to live in Hollywood to make your documentaries. Maybe we live in the mountains. Maybe it's cold year-round. Maybe we have a big house instead of a tiny little apartment. Maybe we have a spare bedroom. Maybe my belly's getting round.

Maybe, maybe, maybe.

I know that it is so much more productive to think about what is instead of what could be.

But there was a part of me that thought getting Lane would be like a test for us.

A test to see if we could handle taking care of another living creature together.

In the six years that I've loved you, K., I've always believed you would be a great dad.

It was myself I was unsure about.

And for a while, I thought that waiting until we were married would be the first step before having a family. I thought you might have asked once we moved here, but it wasn't long after we moved that I got hired full-time at the lab.

Which we both know didn't leave much room for our romantic life.

Sometimes I wonder if you might have planned on asking, that my workload might have given you pause. Sometimes I still wonder if you're moments from asking.

I like to daydream.

I like to think about coming home to a surprise.

But don't worry, K.

I might be the one surprising you with something soon.

Always,

T.

6

JASON WAS STANDING at the window, looking down upon Windward Circle—the statue of Thoth, the Egyptian God, like a guardian beneath Venice Beach's blue skies, and so reminiscent of Margot's paintings—when the house started to shake. The realtor had said it was built to withstand quakes, 'Perfect for raising a family.' Still, Jason crouched under the kitchen table until the rattling ceased. It lasted but thirty seconds, and resulted, Jason was pleased to find, merely in a toppled bookshelf.

He stood and returned to the window, his watchtower since Margot left, to find the Circle draining of its cars and pedestrians—beachgoers, tourists—all in a panic from the tremors. He went to his phone to check social media, but the feeds didn't load; he tried to dial the operator but only heard the busy signal; he went into the study and tapped the trackpad on his laptop—a picture of Margot still set as his wallpaper—but the little Wifi symbol said 'No Connection Available.' He went to the fridge for a beer, and when he opened the door there was no light.

Back at the window, he saw the Circle mostly emptied of people. Except at the base of the statue, beneath Thoth's outstretched hand, stood a child, all alone.

A little girl.

"Where are your parents?" Jason said aloud. He scanned the Circle, but all the people were now gone. Except for the girl. It was like she'd come from nowhere. He waited a few minutes, but no one came for her. She just stood there, as still as the statue above her. It had been months since Jason had left the house—a sabbatical from CavumCorp and dipping into his IRA could afford him as much after what he lost—but he knew that would now have to change if nobody soon claimed this child. He wondered if there was something wrong with her. Could shock have been a minor effect of the quake? Having not thought of such things for over a year now, he didn't know what shock could do to a child. But he couldn't let her stand there unprotected.

He went outside and felt the hot air and sunlight on his skin. Hard to believe there was just an earthquake, he thought. He rounded the building and picked up his pace toward the Circle. When the statue came back into view, he saw the girl standing there stiffly, like something carved from wood. He crossed the street and made a beeline for her. He knelt and got a look at the girl, making sure to keep enough distance as to not frighten her.

"Hi," he said. "I'm Jason. I came over here to make sure you're okay. Where's your mommy and daddy?"

The girl stared at him with wide, gray eyes. She looked to be about five or six, with pale, sickly skin and ash brown hair. Her face looked familiar. Had he seen her somewhere before? Other than with his young cousins before leaving Florida, he had spent very little time in the company of children.

"Can you talk? Can you hear me? You're kind of freaking me out, kid."

She arched her eyebrows. Should he seek out the police, or wait for someone to come and claim her? Supposing no one comes? He looked around, saw a couple across the street, and waved. They gave him a look and kept walking.

He crouched down to the girl. "What's your name, kid? You got a name?" She stared blankly at him, not a trace of a smile. He made faces, wiggled his hands next to his ears, stuck his tongue out, blew a raspberry. She tilted her head like a dog, pouted her lips. Maybe she's mute, he thought. Or deaf-mute. "Can you hear me?" he asked her. "Are you deaf?" She gazed emptily at him.

"Come on," he said and reached for her hand. "I'll walk you to the police station."

He wondered what would cause a child to behave in such a manner. Margot would have known exactly what to do in this situation. She'd had so many stories about her students. He remembered one she'd told him about a boy in her first-grade art class who refused to participate if anybody so much as looked at him. Jason thought it worth a try. He turned around and took a few paces away from the girl. When he peered back, he saw that she'd put one foot forward. He pretended not to see her and kept walking. From the corner of his eye, he saw her take two full steps. Now it was just a matter of getting her to follow him to the station without losing her.

She was several feet from her original spot under the statue. He could pick her up and carry her the two blocks, but at the risk of frightening her. The last thing he needed was her flailing and screaming. Better to make slow, steady progress. Crossing the street from the Circle toward the boardwalk would be difficult, he realized. He stood in the middle of the road and looked back. She was about to take her first step onto the pavement. No way, he thought. What kind of person lets a child cross the street, even a currently barren one, alone?

"Come on," he said, reaching down to gently grab her hand, so cold in his. He expected her to retract, or run, but she let him guide her to the other side without trouble. Now that he had her moving, he kept his gait slow and steady. He wondered what he was going to say to the police once he got to the station. Would they think he was some kind of abductor? Probably not, but he figured they'd have to keep him around for questioning. The station came into view as he rounded the corner. People filed out of the building, onto the street. The girl stopped walking and started to turn back for the Circle.

"Whoa, wait a minute," he said. She tried to pull free. "It's okay, little one. Don't be afraid." He tightened his hand for fear of her running away. Was it some dormant fatherly instinct kicking in? It didn't take much effort; she felt weak for her size. But what did he know about children, other than the eight weeks he'd spent reading parenting books? She turned her head and looked into his eyes. He realized of whom the girl had reminded him. Margot, or at least the version of her he'd seen in childhood photos: same downy chin, flat lips, wide eyes—though the child's were a mysterious gray color. Could be a side-effect of malnutrition, he reasoned.

"You've got to come with me," he said. "We have to get you some help." He felt silly for trying to talk to her. Her expression went unchanged, a constant lack of emotion. Venice had now begun to grow dark, yet the streetlamps emitted no light. Surely the city must have backup generators,

Jason thought. He had to get the kid into proper care before things got worse. "Please. I need you to cooperate with me." To his surprise, the girl's hand went limp. "Okay," said Jason. "Good. There's nothing to worry about. We're going to find your family soon."

When he turned, the crowd outside the station had grown. He guided the girl forward until they were within the first few rows of people. They were an even mixture, Jason could now see, of business owners, residents, tourists, and the homeless. The more he cautiously waded deeper toward the station, the clearer the gatherers' thrum of complaints became.

"Our whole building is without power."

"Try the whole block!"

While most of the gatherers' concerns pertained to the outage, several people clustered around the outside of the crowd, pointing wildly toward the beach.

"A sinkhole!" they shouted.

"Split the boardwalk in two!"

Jason, gripping the girl tighter, stood tall and tried to see over the crowd. He thought of the sinkholes he'd seen in Florida—water main breaks bad enough to destroy homes and roads. But could they form in Los Angeles, where it hardly ever rained? Geologically, it made no sense. But if not a sinkhole, what on earth had these people seen?

Just as Jason felt the panic rise in and around him, an officer came out of the station and triggered a warning alarm until the crowd's attention was on him. "We've heard your concerns," he said through a megaphone. Jason felt the girl pull her hand from his. When he looked down, she was covering her ears. "So far, we know all of Venice and Santa Monica are without power. That's at least ten thousand homes. We expect additional assistance very soon. We are doing everything possible to ensure the safety of our citizens, including evacuating the beach and boardwalk. We ask that, unless you have an emergency, you please cooperate and return to your places of dwelling."

The crowd pulsed around Jason and the girl. As a few of them trickled away, Jason felt that finding the girl's parents *was* an emergency. They had the right to bypass the others. He tried to push forward, the girl clinging to his side and going stiff, but the crowd enclosed tighter around them. He hoisted the girl into his arms, relieved she didn't writhe or try to break away. With force, he started to make progress. Maybe they could see in his eyes the fire of a father, the look on his face that said, 'I will die for this child.' Maybe it was her resemblance to Margot, but he felt acutely protective of the child. At the front of the crowd, with all the people finally behind them, he set the girl on her feet.

"Please," Jason said to the officer. "I just found this girl without her parents. I waited with her, but no one came. I think there's something wrong with her."

The officer gave the girl one look. He told Jason to follow him into the station and shut the door behind them.

"Normally, we let Child Protective Services handle these matters, but with no phone…" The officer shrugged. "Here's what I'd do." He scribbled something on a memo pad. "There's a social services agency six blocks from here. I say take her there. Otherwise, God knows how long it'll be before I can free up an officer to walk her over." He tore the memo off and handed it to Jason. "I'm sorry, but it's the best I can do right now."

Jason didn't know what to say. Of what use were the police if not in matters such as this? A conundrum of privilege, he was well aware. But what the hell was he supposed to do? He picked up the girl again and cradled her over his shoulder. He didn't put her down until they were outside, beyond the crowd. Nightfall had come, and Jason could barely read the address the officer had written on the scrap of paper. Traffic had increased since earlier, grown more chaotic, and headlights were now the only means by which to navigate. Jason knew it would be futile trying to get the girl to the social services building like this. He'd done the right thing; he'd tried to get help from law enforcement, but the law failed them. He had no other option.

"Let's go," he said, taking her hand and guiding her away from the crowds. "We have no choice but to try in the morning." It was so dark now he couldn't see her face, only her wide, gray eyes shimmering in the moonlight. He led her around the corner and past Windward Circle. When they got to the house, she needed a little help getting up the stairs. Once they were inside, she stood in the living room while he built a fort out of blankets.

"It's all yours," Jason said. "Test it out while I make you something to eat." He handed her a water bottle from the side table. She stared, no movement. "Right. I'll have to get you a straw, I guess."

He started for the kitchen and, checking over his shoulder, saw her turned toward the fort. To prepare a proper snack upstairs was tough, considering the power outage. Downstairs, he'd stockpiled goods for such an occasion, but he was able to make oatmeal with blueberries.

"I also have peanut butter and jelly," he said, heading back to the living room, "but I can't be sure you don't have allergies."

The child was gone. Jason saw the fort's front flap shaking. With the bowl of oatmeal and spoon in one hand and the water bottle in the other, he shimmied on his knees to the fort and looked inside to see her sitting there, cross-legged.

"I see you've made yourself comfortable."

He reached in and placed the oatmeal and water bottle in front of her.

"You got to eat this, okay? If you don't eat it, you'll get sick. We don't want that, now, do we?"

The child's eyes lowered to the food, but she didn't move. With a sigh, Jason dragged himself deeper into the tent, until he was far enough to lift a spoonful of oats and hold it close to her lips. She opened her mouth. He fed her the oats. Her mouth hung open. He put his hand under her chin and moved her jaw to emulate chewing. After three assisted chews, she finally got the hang of it. Her cheeks were puffed. She coughed. What if she starts choking? he wondered, watching her. He was trying to remember how to do CPR when the girl took the spoon from him and dug it deep into the bowl, excavating a blueberry, which she plucked and held up with her fingers.

"A blueberry," said Jason, smiling.

With a giggle the girl returned his smile, then she plunged the blueberry into her mouth. Juice from it dribbled down her chin. With a clatter she dropped the spoon and fed the rest of the oats to herself by the handful, shoveling them into her face until the bowl was empty. Having scraped the bowl clean with her fingers she threw it at Jason, who put up his hand and flinched. He looked up to see her smiling at him with oats smeared across her face.

"I think that's enough for now," he said. "Here, have some water."

He handed her the water bottle from which a curly straw protruded.

"You need to stay hydrated." As if she knew what 'hydrated' meant. As if she knew the word 'water.' As if she knew any words. She eyed the straw curiously, gave it a flick with her tongue.

"That's it," said Jason.

She picked up the bottle and turned it over. Water cascaded down her shirt.

"Damn," Jason said.

He crawled out of the tent and went to get a wash towel. When he returned, he found the child lying asleep on her side. As best he could, he wiped her face. He gave her a pillow and a blanket. As he stood looking down at the tent, the snoring sounds emanating from inside it brought to mind an animal, some furry wild creature rescued from deep in the woods, an injured raccoon or bear cub. Where had she come from? How could someone lose a child like that? He recalled the time when, more than anything else, he'd wanted a child of his own, the joy that had surged through him when Margot told him she was pregnant, how the thought of being a father had made him feel complete. When Margot lost the baby, he had been ready to try again. But she couldn't get over that loss. I should have married her, he thought, watching the tent swell and contract with the child's breathing. Maybe then she wouldn't have left.

He checked the locks on all the doors and windows and cleaned some broken glass from a framed photograph of him and Margot that must have fallen during the quake. Once he was sure the house was secured and childproofed, he took out a local map and the paper with the address to social services. The agency was located two miles north of the house, which would be exhausting without a car. In the morning, he'd pack a bag to prepare for the trek. He wondered if the girl would fit in the stroller he'd bought prematurely. There were so many baby things downstairs he'd never use, all purchased with blind optimism. One thing he hadn't bought was a car seat, and he didn't think it safe to drive her without one. He figured the girl was too big for the stroller meant for a newborn, that he'd have to carry her to social services.

He lay in front of the fort because he didn't want the girl to get scared if she woke up and couldn't find him. He wondered if he had done the right thing, bringing her to his house. But what else could he have done, given the circumstances? Pretended not to see her at all, or left her at the police station? It just didn't feel right, leaving her there when the officer had made it sound like she wouldn't have gotten the proper help she needed. He told himself that bringing her back to the house was what Margot would have done. She would never have left the girl in someone else's hands.

In the darkness of the house, he lay wondering what Margot and her husband were doing at that moment. She lived in Hollywood now—the one place where she'd sworn to never reside—in her husband's apartment. Jason had gathered this much from a few of their mutual friends, as well as other more disconcerting details: the death of Margot's husband's ex-girlfriend, for one. Jason couldn't fathom such a thing. He'd heard the woman had done it in the apartment. Jason had heard she was some kind of scientist, an important figure in her field. He'd often wondered what was so special about this guy, Margot's husband. What qualities in him could make a woman take her life? What had Margot found in this guy that Jason didn't have?

He hadn't communicated with Margot since she'd left. He tried, but she either blocked his phone number or ignored him. When he'd seen—vis-à-vis mutual friends on social media—that she eloped with the guy after knowing him only two weeks, well, Jason had wanted to crawl into a hole and die. Secluding himself in the house for months had been his way of doing just that. He'd bought the house, after all. He wasn't just going to move back to Florida. So long as he pulled his weight at CavumCorp after his sabbatical, he'd have no reason to go back to the infernal humidity, the stagnant and often complacent mode of existence. As far as everyone back home was concerned, he was living the dream: Six figures, beachside paradise, bachelor's lifestyle. At least, this was the life he projected online. Hell, based on the number of likes his posts received, his life was the envy of the Treasure Coast. Sure, some of his old friends had reached out with condolences when news of the separation went public. But none of them had known about the baby, so he was able to keep the conversations short, chalk it up to "for the best."

But he knew his solitude served only as a fleeting asylum.

His hope: The longer he stayed in the house, the more any memories of Margot's presence would evaporate.

His truth: As long as he remained, she'd know where to find him.

Inside the fort, the little girl's snoring had grown louder. Jason wondered what would have come of the girl if he hadn't seen her, if he'd left Venice when Margot moved. And what if Margot hadn't lost the baby? Would he have ever crossed paths with the girl?

Moonbeams pierced the window overlooking Windward Circle. From where Jason lay, he saw the girl's face. She was peacefully asleep. Had he imagined her resemblance to Margot? Had he projected Margot's likeness onto her? Lying on the floor, he tried to remember if he still had one of Margot's old photo albums stashed away in the basement. He thought of the baby and all the unused things. He thought of the empty shell of a house. He watched a cloud drift over the moon, shrouding the house in total darkness. Jason kept his eyes open until, like the child, he was overpowered by sleep.

When he opened his eyes, the girl stood over him holding the oatmeal bowl, her head tilted to one side and her eyes still narrow. Through the slants between her eyelids, Jason saw the pale gray of her irises glimmering.

"You're hungry," he said. "That's a good sign." He stood up, stretched, and took the bowl before making his way into the kitchen. "We'll get you fed and then it's off to social services. I can't take care of you long-term. This was a one-time thing." The girl had followed behind him, staring with awe as he rinsed the bowl, poured in fresh oats, boiled water, and stirred it together. He had to keep the bowl from her, so eager to eat the steaming oats. A chocolate bar sat on the counter, but when he refused her effort to grab it, she pouted and went back into the living room. He followed her and, when the bowl cooled, put it on the table. He handed her a spoon and demonstrated how to use it. She again reached in to scoop the oats with her hand.

While the girl ate, Jason checked the house for power. Still no signs of electricity. When he tried his phone and the Internet, there was no signal or connection. He went to the window, his watchtower, and looked down at Windward Circle. His neighborhood, and what he could see of Venice Beach, was mostly absent of the typical traffic and bustle, surfers and beachgoers. A few stragglers walked alone, in stride, but this was a far cry from the tourist trap to which he'd grown accustomed. He turned back to the girl and watched her finish eating. When the bowl was empty, she just sat at the table and stared out the window. Jason stood beside her and put his finger on the glass, pointing out to the statue of Thoth.

"See that there? That's where I found you. Do you remember that?" He knelt and looked at her face: peaceful and serene, but impassive. He waved his hand and snapped his fingers, trying to get her to look at him, but she didn't budge. He went to the kitchen for the candy bar and, when he returned, tore the wrapper in front of her. She turned when it crinkled, but only showed minimal interest. Now her eyes were locked on the statue. She lifted her hand and put it to the window. A sound came from her, barely audible—a low humming. Jason watched her lips move and eyebrows twitch.

"Mome," she said, tapping the glass. "Mo. Mome."

"Mome?" Jason was relieved to finally hear her voice, sweet and soft but scratchy from lack of use. "What are you trying to say?"

"Mome," she repeated. She looked up at him. "Mome. Go mome."

Go home—she was saying Go Home.

"Okay, so you can speak," Jason said, crouching beside her. "Now we're getting somewhere. You want to go home? I understand that, little one. And I'm going to try to help you. Do you understand that?"

She took her finger away from the glass and planted herself back down in the chair.

She reached for the chocolate bar, nearly falling out of her chair. "Whoa, there. All you had to do was ask." He broke off a piece and handed it to her. She held it out, examined it, and crammed it in her mouth. He watched her chew the chocolate with her mouth open, making sure she didn't choke. When she was finished, he cleaned the smudges from her face and started preparing for the trek. He packed a light travel bag with minimal first aid supplies, dried fruit, and water. He guided her out of the house, step by step down the stairs, until they were back on the ground, the morning sun beaming over their heads.

Jason wasn't sure if he should try the police station again or go straight for social services. He held her hand as they crossed the street to Windward Circle and kept her at arm's length when they neared the statue. He bent and searched the dirt where she had stood. Her footprints remained, but there were no other traces of her. A plate mounted at the bottom of the statue caught Jason's eye. Leaning closer, he read the words engraved in the metal: 'All which exists is only another form of that which exists not.'

The girl stood at his side with her finger pointed at Thoth.

"Mome," she said. "Gome home."

With her other hand, she reached for Jason's sleeve and gave it a slight tug.

"Alright," he told her. He stood, the statue towering over him, and took her hand. "Let's get you home."

He started in the direction of the social services building—he could see from the Circle a new crowd of people outside the police station. He didn't want to waste any more time. When he looked down to check on the girl, he saw her peering back toward the statue, waving goodbye to it.

The further they walked down the block, the more people Jason saw near the boardwalk entrance. Police tape had been put up to keep people away from the cleft in the ground, but it wasn't working. If he didn't know any better, he'd have thought the cleft a new attraction, like the Freakshow—which Margot hated—sans ushers to guide people on a tour. People clustered around the gaping hole in the ground with their phones, taking pictures of it. Fools, Jason thought. From where he and the girl stood, he saw the tip of a bulge in the pavement and the opening of a crater that extended into the sand. He wondered how such a cavity could be possible in this landscape. Artificially drained swampland was one thing, but here? In a place so dry? There had to be another explanation. Though he wanted to get closer, he knew a detour would be unfair—and unsafe—for the girl, that every passing moment was a lost opportunity to return her to those who had lost her.

No sooner than he started north again did he hear the screaming. He looked over to the cleft and saw people on their hands and knees, calling into the chasm. A moment later, groups of people separated, running off in different directions. The screaming continued, getting louder, coming from inside the crater. Jason felt the girl tugging his hand, trying to get away from him. But she wasn't trying to run away from the crater or the screaming. She wanted to run toward it. Her squirming turned into a desperate attempt, with all her strength, to break free. She looked up at him, the vacant expression she'd worn now wild, almost feral. And her eyes, their usual light gray, were flickering with white. A trick of the light? Jason wondered. When her hand slipped out of his, he reached for her, but she took off running at a speed Jason hadn't anticipated. He dropped the supply bag and chased her, against the onslaught of people rushing toward them, in the direction of the chasm.

MARGOT HAD FELT the change during the drive home. That they could not leave the city had instilled in Margot unshakable anxiety. The baby, the power, the growing sense of doom—she had control over nothing, and Knox could not calm her, try as he might. Both of them were at a loss; even Lane lay across the backseat, silent and deflated. As Knox drove back toward The Libra, Margot fought the urge to bring up Jason. She kept her mouth shut as they passed the Hollywood Forever Cemetery, where tents were lined up outside the gate as they had been at the Silver Lake Reservoir. The cemetery's gates were chained, but Margot saw people climbing over, desperate to get to the other side. What shelter could they have expected to find for themselves there, amongst the dead? She put her hand on Knox's lap. He kept his gaze focused on the road ahead, both hands on the steering wheel. She tried to remember the dreams she'd invented for herself upon moving to LA. Becoming an artist? Selling her paintings on the boardwalk? Opening a gallery? It all seemed so trivial, so childishly naive now that she had left the man for whom she moved here and become a full-time elementary school teacher. In the face of despair, the illusion of Los Angeles as a place of endless opportunities had faded, as had her willingness to chase fantasies. How could someone raise a child in a city so derelict? Even in Beverly Hills and Malibu, where they could never afford to live on her teacher's salary in addition to Knox's tips and inconsistent freelancing, people had their versions of disuse and neglect; Margot had learned from Jason that having money doesn't necessarily make a person more sensible. The last she'd heard of Jason, from a mutual friend, he hadn't left the house in months. Assuming he had any sense, Margot thought, he would have sold the house and buried the past, as she had done.

As Knox turned onto Vine, Margot noticed the normal tourists and costumed characters were nowhere to be seen. The street was full of police cars and fire trucks, their blue and red lights flickering across the front of the Jane Fonda Theatre and the Museum of Death. Margot sat up and looked around for the source of the commotion but couldn't see over a pair of ambulances to her right. Lane shifted in back, pressing his paws against the window while Knox tried to maneuver around the blockade preventing them from getting to The Libra. Margot reached to pet Lane, trying to calm him, but the flashing lights had made him inconsolable. She could also sense Knox's growing frustration, his silence a tell-all whenever he felt helpless. She wanted to comfort him, despite what was going on outside. She was his wife, wasn't she? They both needed assurance that they weren't alone in this.

"I've got an idea," she said, running her hand up his thigh. "What if when we get upstairs, we cuddle and forget the world for a while?"

Knox looked at her. He smiled, put his hand on hers, and puckered his lips. She leaned in and kissed him. When their lips touched, she longed to go back to the way things were, their year of marriage now like a deeply buried time capsule. The kiss was fleeting, Knox's attention soon drawn back to navigating the Jeep around the block. From her new vantage point, Margot saw the cause of all the sirens; two blocks away from The Libra, in the middle of Hollywood Boulevard, lay a row of people—bodies. Paramedics covered them with a white tarpaulin.

Margot felt the bile rise.

"What happened?" she said. "We've only been gone a few hours."

As Knox turned into The Libra's parking lot, he slowed the Jeep and looked beyond Margot toward the boulevard.

His face had gone pale.

"They're dead," he said.

Margot said nothing.

"How many were there?" Knox asked.

She'd counted the bumps in the tarpaulin. "Maybe a dozen."

Knox pulled into their parking spot, turned off the engine, and bit his knuckle. Margot's face felt suddenly hot. Tears welled up and rolled down her cheek. Seeing them, Knox reached to cup the back of her head in his hand. She looked into his eyes and saw he was crying, too. At the sight of this, Lane lunged between them and trilled, his tongue lapping at their faces as if trying to erase their tears. Margot put one arm around the dog and the other around Knox. She held them tight, afraid that once she let them go, they'd be gone for good, prone to the dangers outside. Knox reached under her shirt and pressed his hand to her stomach.

"Let's go upstairs," he said. "We're going to barricade ourselves in the apartment. When we run out of food and water, I'll be the one to go get more. We're going to ride this thing out until it gets better."

"And what if it doesn't get better?" Margot said.

"It has to."

She nodded and pushed her face into his neck, drying her eyes on his shirt. She wanted to believe him, that all the hysteria would disappear in a few days.

K.,

The first experiment for RIFT was a failure. Mind you—it was never intended to be a success.

This is why we call them experiments.

However, as far as failures go, this one was rather severe.

Our collider is a twenty-three-mile machine beneath Los Angeles, California.

Something like this was bound to happen eventually. I'm just surprised a team of physicists couldn't foresee it. But, like Tajū said, after a while, it's hard to see the forest for the trees.

Essentially, what one of my earlier simulations failed to predict was the seismic effect of the gravitational force from the collision. You don't need me to tell you the outcome. Thankfully, it was minimal considering what our collider is capable of. The company has enough money to mask the cause from the public eye. The only thing that gets reported is the magnitude. Luckily, ours was only a magnitude of four. Enough for people to feel it, but not enough to draw too much attention to ourselves.

Tajū has been forgiving, although I can't help but feel embarrassment around the rest of the team. I need you right now. I want to call, but you're working. Now I know how you feel when I can't answer. Down in the lab, I sometimes feel as if I'm in Plato's Cave, a witness to mere shadows of what is real.

Lately, I spend too much time contemplating the aspects and truths about what is real and what is not, K.

You can only contemplate reality so much until your own reality begins to seem unreal. When this happens, the best remedy I can find is to think deeply and specifically about my identity.

Who are you, Tiffany?

I am a young woman from Ohio. An Ohioan at heart. A Toledoan in spirit. I'm the daughter of Terri, a baker, and Lewis, a musician. I learned from them many things, but I became a physicist, something neither of them could have predicted. I grew up a bit sheltered. I loved my books. I didn't get out much. I didn't have a boyfriend until college when I met an amazing guy at a stupid party. I am happy to say that he is the love of my life. I am a person who loves movies. I am a person who loves science. I am a person who wants a family. I am a person who wants to be a wife. I am a person who wants to be a mother. I am a person who is deeply afraid that these things will not come to pass due to my investment in my work. I am a person who is capable of making mistakes just like anyone.

I am a person who should not be so hard on herself.

I digress.

In a moment, I'm leaving for a meeting about a proposed addition to our collider that can aim to accomplish what the LHC could not. Meanwhile, Tajū has had a separate team working night and day on a new project called Democritus. Now that it's completed, he is soon to be releasing a statement about what will henceforth be known as the Radial Fermion Expander. It has been shown that the LHC could not produce a black hole big enough to sustain Hawking radiation. It would take the black hole trillions of years to expand to a sustainable size. Tajū's expander will reduce that time to a mere three hundred sixty-five days. He believes this can succeed where my experiment failed. I'll try to keep my chin up in front of the team.

My father used to tell me that the purpose of life was to get up, fall, and get up again knowing that another fall is inevitable. He used to say it was a cycle we are never meant to escape.

If that's true, then I just have to get up from this. I must trust myself and put my best foot forward.

Sometimes it's the only thing we can do.

8

WHEN KNOX TURNED the key and pushed the door, it banged against the security chain. He looked at Margot, whose shock must have mirrored his own. Who could have possibly been in their apartment? Had he given someone the key? Had Tiffany or Margot done so? His gut gurgled, his pulse raced. Margot was right. They never should have left The Libra.

"Let's just get out of here," Margot said. "Please."

"This is our home."

He backed away from the door and held his hand up to Margot, signaling for her to give him space. "Open the door," he said, voice loud enough for the whole floor to hear. "Open it or I'm going to kick it in."

"I wouldn't do that if I were you, Mr. Everett," a man said from inside the apartment. The voice sounded familiar. "You kick this door in, you and your wife are going to regret it." Margot cocked her head, her eyes pleading. The man inside shoved the door closed, and Knox could hear him bolt the lock. That's when he realized to whom the voice belonged—the man who had knocked on their door before they left, the one who had said he and four other guys were with the FBI. The man must have learned his name from the mail stacked on the kitchen counter.

What else could this guy know about us? he thought. Knox had packed most of their important paperwork when they left—their marriage license, birth certificates, social security cards. He told himself not to get intimidated if the man used any more personal information against them. He checked his pocket, feeling around for the mace. He'd taken it without telling Margot. It was their only weapon.

"I'm getting the police. For your sake, you'd better be gone when they get here."

"Good luck with that," the man said.

Were all of the guys who'd posed as feds inside their apartment?

"I'm sure you're not as dumb as you look," the man continued. "The police aren't going to be much help to you right now. They've got enough on their hands. By the time they get here, we'll be long gone."

Knox tensed the muscles in his legs, ready to break down the door. He felt rage coursing through his body, the desire to reclaim his territory blinding him.

"Please," Margot repeated, her voice low enough for Knox alone to hear. "Let's just go." Even in the dark Knox saw her trembling, Lane's leash wrapped taught around her hand. The dog had been growling, protecting Margot from the potential harm on the other side of the door. Knox unclenched his fist, took the leash from Margot, and guided Lane down the corridor, to the stairs. He needed to get out of The Libra before his rage caused him to make an irredeemable mistake, putting his life and Margot's in jeopardy. She was close behind him, her hand on his shirt as if she'd lose him.

Once outside, Knox guided her into the Jeep, started the engine, and pressed his foot down hard on the gas pedal. He hadn't even buckled his seatbelt when the side of the vehicle scraped against the building on the way to the street.

Note:

Came home for a few days to spend time with K.

Wanted to propose.

Wanted to tell him I'm late.

While he was cooking, I saw his phone light up.

A text. From another woman. Her name is Margot.

Couldn't help myself. I took his phone, hid in the bedroom, and tried to read everything. There were only a few texts. At first, I didn't think much of it—maybe it was someone from work. But my jealousy was rampant. I logged into his Facebook to check his messages. I typed in her name and found a string of conversations.

I don't know what to do.

Don't know what to think.

I wanted to ask him about it, but I couldn't bring myself to do it. This is the last thing I need right now with everything going on here.

9

MARGOT GRIPPED THE dashboard. “Can you please slow down?”

“They must have been waiting for us to leave,” Knox said. “They asked if it was just us in the apartment. They watched us. They spied on us, invaded our home. How did they get in without a key?”

“They probably picked the lock.” She looked at the floor mat, afraid of their speed and seeing more bodies under the tarpaulin. “It doesn’t matter. That guy was right. We can’t go to the police.”

“We can try.”

“And say what?” For a moment he didn’t answer. “You know we don’t have another option.”

Behind them, Lane cried—Margot realized she’d tuned him out since leaving The Libra. She looked back and saw shame in the dog’s expression, a dripping puddle beneath him.

“We’ll find somewhere else to go,” Knox said.

“The dog just pissed in the back seat,” Margot said. “There is nowhere else to go.”

He let his foot off the gas. “I don’t know if I can face him.”

She sat up, put both hands on his leg. "You're going to have to."

He turned away.

"It's not like I want to see him again," she continued. "When I left, I didn't even give him an explanation. I just vanished. You were my escape, my reason to forget the past. Sure, I could have sat with him and explained my plan to leave—but I didn't feel a need to. I'd already chosen you."

He remained silent. She tried not to stare, giving him what space she could. While he drove, she wondered if you can ever truly vanish from another's life. Although the baby hadn't been born, it still felt like a part of Margot, suppressed as those feelings had been over the past year. Now: a new baby, a second baby. Could she blend the memories of the two pregnancies, trick her mind into believing the miscarriage never happened? She wondered if Knox had done that with her and Tiffany, if his memories of the past year overlapped with those of the six before. Tiffany, after all, hadn't vanished from Knox's life—she'd vanished from the world. Though not entirely, Margot thought. There was still her note. After the therapist urged them to burn it, Margot told Knox she would dispose of it, but, when the time came, couldn't bring herself to strike the match. Instead, she read the note again a dozen times, mouthing the words, a code she couldn't decipher, before taping it to the back of a canvas in the walk-in closet.

Why couldn't she let Tiffany vanish? What had compelled her to bring the note along when Knox told her to pack for Glendale? Maybe the future is the synthesis of the past and present, she thought, one hand on her stomach, the other on Knox's knee. If the power hadn't gone out, if the quake hadn't happened, what would she have done about the pregnancy? Would she and Knox have argued through the night? Come morning, would she have gone to the clinic? The thought of being without the baby made her nauseated—or was it the violation of invaders, the displacement, the sight of the dead bodies, the smell of dog urine?

She dug her fingers into Knox's thigh. He winced, squeezed her hand.

"You okay?"

She shook her head. "Going to be sick."

Knox pulled over. She opened her door and leaned outside. The fresh air in her lungs abated the urge to puke. She needed to step out, put her feet on solid ground. She heard Knox's door shut, the dog's paws on concrete. They came around to her, and Knox put his hand on her back.

"We'll go to Jason's," he said. "You're right. It's our only choice."

She nodded.

"I'll let Lane do his business and then clean up the car. After that, we'll go to Venice."

"You're sure?"

"I'm sure."

He knelt, kissed the top of her head, and walked Lane down the block. She sat on the cement and cradled her knees, feeling the ground firm beneath her. She summoned the instructions from so many meditation videos she'd seen on the Internet: focus on the breath, focus on where the body makes contact with the earth, and embrace its support. She wondered how valid this advice was, considering the recent fallout from the quake. At any moment, the world beneath us can rumble and change everything, she thought. At this moment, though, at this minuscule point in time, my world is still—immovable.

Dear K.,

I just want you to know that I know.

I know, and I'm struggling with it, and I'm in a lot of pain but I'm learning to numb myself to it with my work.

I want to go home, back to Ohio, to my parents.

But I don't feel as though I should be the one to have to leave.

I worked hard to get where I am.

I don't want to leave this place because of you.

This place that was supposed to be ours.

This place was our dream. What we had worked toward for years.

It's shocking how easily, how quickly, it can all be swept away.

I want to say that I can't blame you. I want to blame my distance. But I can't return home for fear of shame. I won't let my parents see what a fool you've made of me. I won't allow you to have such power over me.

The funny thing is I don't even know if I have the power to send this to you.

I just don't know if there is a point in trying anymore.

Why bother when I've already lost you?

JASON SPRINTED AFTER the girl. Where had she summoned such speed? He weaved through a wall of people rushing toward him, fearing he would find her trampled. Having knocked him over, the crowds dispersed down side streets, into alleys. Jason locked eyes on the girl as she ran up the now abandoned boardwalk. So close to the cleft, the girl slowed and turned around. She pointed at the ground, and he picked up speed, desperate to reach her before she took a step too far.

With the splitting ground in view, Jason ran onto the sand and struggled to keep his balance. Shards of rock jutted from the earth, the size of footballs. A few yards away, the girl stood still, as she had beneath the statue of Thoth, her pointer finger stretched out toward what Jason saw—an abyss, a lack of sand and earth.

Jason wrapped his arm around the girl and pulled her away from the chasm. She let out a sound as if wounded. He tightened his hands on her shoulders. "What's wrong with you, kid? You trying to get yourself killed?" The volume of his voice shook her, the gray in her eyes shimmering like rays of light dancing on water. She wrestled against his hands, looking past him toward the chasm. If he let her go, she'd make a run for it. What was it in the hole, drawing her, calling to her?

He picked her up, swung her onto his back, and held her hands to his chest. Though she kept wriggling, he had secured her enough to take a few steps toward the gorge. His feet shifted in the sand, unable to keep proper balance without his hands. Within arm's reach of the hole, he leaned forward and peered inside.

What had made all those people scream? When he first heard them, he assumed someone had fallen in. But what would have sent everyone running? Whatever it was, could it still linger in the darkness, out of his periphery? Did the girl know what lurked down the cavernous hole?

He stepped closer and saw, barely visible, a thin line radiating with violet light. Visible only when he squinted, the line was no bigger than a crack in an egg. It pulsed—light, then dark, and light again. Violet to black, violet to black.

The girl squirmed, her hands and knees thrashing against Jason's torso.

"Mome," she said. "Gome home!"

The light throbbed, growing brighter with each palpitation.

"Let's go," Jason said.

He took a step backward. The girl writhed. He fought to contain her, her strength surprising him. His ankle suddenly folded, his foot without friction atop the fast-sifting sand. She tried to pull her hands free. He bent a knee and wrapped his arms around her. He got to his feet, vulnerable to her pummeling limbs.

She's good as dead if I let her go, he thought.

As he tried to turn away from the crater, his eyes fixated on the darkness, the faint glow of violet much brighter than before, and larger—a beacon signaling him.

Everything went silent. The world enveloped in shade.

He felt a wave of cold air against his skin. He exhaled, saw his breath. It would have been so easy, submitting to the frigid dark within the hole, its promise of entombment like a deep sleep for which he hungered. If not for the girl wildly thrashing in his arms, he might have fallen under the spell of the chasm, the violet light pulling him nearer until he plunged into the abyss.

Wake up, he thought. *Wake up, Jason.*

The Venice Beach sunlight returned, wiping away the darkness. It blinded him as he ran, the girl in his arms weightless after his kick of adrenaline. He trudged through the sand and leaped over a gap dividing the beach from the boardwalk. Landing on the cement, he embraced the impact with his knee. Pain shot through his leg, but he stood and limped, still holding the girl, until they reached Windward Circle. As soon as he put her down, she walked, on her own, toward the house. He limped behind her, trying to keep up, afraid he wouldn't have the strength to catch her if she tried to run again.

11

KNOX LET MARGOT guide him past the canals, where he and Tiffany used to walk for hours. Compared to those in Hollywood, the streets of Venice were placid. Margot pointed to a roundabout and told him to park anywhere he could find a space. Among other vehicles jettisoned by their owners, misaligned along the curbs, choices for the Jeep were few. He paralleled into a too-small spot and left the Jeep there, its nose sticking out.

"That's the place," she said, nodding toward a periwinkle two-story house. He knew she'd lived in Venice with Jason, but he had never picked her up, dropped her off, or been near her home. Whenever they'd met, it had been at a coffee shop or bar. She'd vent about her relationship with Jason, claiming he was possessive, overbearing, that he disapproved of her leaving the house. The picture she painted in Knox's mind had been one of a woman in an abusive relationship. He wondered how much of that had been true. After all, she'd never once said anything about being pregnant, or that she and Jason had just lost a child. How had he not seen the signs? In her eagerness to detach from that part of her life, had she hidden all signs of her trauma?

He hadn't exactly been honest with her, either. He'd said nothing about Tiffany, or that he was in a relationship, until weeks after meeting Margot.

"You ready?" she asked.

Lane's head perked up, his tail thumping against the seat. Perhaps he sensed they were at the beach, anticipating fetch in the sand like they'd done when Tiffany was alive.

"As I'll ever be," he answered. He reached back to scratch Lane's chin. The dog's tongue hung out, expressing a joy Knox envied. Margot opened her door, walked around the Jeep, and stood by the driver's side.

"Can we leave Lane in the car for now?" she said.

Knox nodded. He cracked the windows and turned off the engine. As he got out, his heart raced, the periwinkle house proof of the life he could never give Margot. He had taken her from a life of luxury, he thought, to a barren one-bedroom apartment. How could he ever give her what this guy had?

As Lane whined in the Jeep, Margot took her first steps toward the house. Knox followed, his gaze locked on the large windows overlooking the roundabout. He imagined Margot up there, easel set up, surrounded by paints and brushes. She had probably spent hours looking out that window. He'd often wondered how it must have felt to exist in the world of her paintings. And now here they were, walking through one of her landscapes.

He followed her through the yard. She ignored the front door and headed straight for the back. He noticed the neighboring houses nearby—no lights, sounds, or signs of electricity. How far did the outage reach? They climbed a staircase leading to the second level of the house, and Margot knocked on the door.

"Maybe he's not here," Knox said. "He could have left before things got too bad."

"Something tells me he didn't leave."

She put her face to the window, cupped her hands over her eyes. Knox checked to see if anyone was watching them, suddenly aware of how suspect they looked. He heard Margot jiggle the door handle—locked. From the top of the stairwell, he saw someone walking around the house, a man with a child at his side. Before Knox could get Margot's attention, the man saw them and stopped.

"Margot?" the man said. "What are you doing here?"

Jason, Knox thought. But who is the kid?

Margot stepped to the edge of the stairwell.

"I know it's sudden," she said. "But we have nowhere else to go. They're not letting anyone out of the city. Our phones don't work, and people invaded our home."

Jason stood before the child—a little girl?—blocking it from view.

"We haven't spoken in a year," he said.

"I know. I'm sorry."

The child peeked around Jason's arm. Knox couldn't help but look, locking eyes with the child. Her eyes—remarkably bright, familiar.

"This isn't the best time," Jason said.

"Whose child is that?" Margot asked.

Knox and the girl kept eye contact, her gaze adrift, detached.

"It's hard to explain," Jason said. Behind him, the girl tried to step away, her eyes on Margot now, an abrupt show of curiosity on her face.

"Momma," the girl said. She tried to break free from Jason, but he held her back. An animal sound, like a cat's mewing, erupted from her mouth.

"I need you to try," Margot insisted.

"Upstairs," said Jason. "Step aside so I can get her in. Okay?"

Knox looked to Margot. She nodded, took his hand, and made room for them to walk past. Slowly, Jason guided the girl up the stairs. Once at the top, he walked in front of Knox without a sign of acknowledgment. The girl, however, peered up at him—those eyes still shining, almost silvery.

"Momma," she said again and reached for Margot's hand.

Margot pulled away.

"What's wrong with her?"

"We'll talk in the house," Jason said.

He unlocked the door and walked inside, leaving it open for Margot and Knox. Margot cocked her eyebrow at Knox and followed them. Left alone on the stairs, Knox surveyed the area once more. The bright sun, the blue sky—he knew things would never be normal again.

He stepped into Jason's house and closed the door.

K.,

Second experiment—another failure.

This time I don't know if it's one I can spring back from.

What I can say is that there was no quake this time. I've learned how to avoid it and what would cause it to happen again.

This time, you might have noticed that for seventy-four minutes last night there was no power in East LA.

What you might not have guessed is that RIFT had everything to do with it.

Lately, I just can't get it together.

The company couldn't hide this one from the public. Another slip like this could allow the government to shut us down, which would be the end of my career as we know it.

Might not be the worst thing.

I've got one more shot with the collider before Tajū finds my replacement. He told me that he doesn't want to, but that we must do what is best for the collider.

Seems like a lack of me is what would be best all around, lately.

12

BEING INSIDE THE house again made Margot shaky. She looked around the kitchen, many of her decorations still hanging, even one of her paintings—an oceanside view of the boardwalk with souvenir shops on the right, independent artists and vendors on the left. She'd been so proud of it, her first painting after moving out west.

"Don't mind the mess," Jason said. "The maid hasn't been by in a while."

What mess? Margot thought. The place was still nearly impeccable, a show of his obsessive need to keep all things in their place. The rumors must have been true. He hadn't left this place in months. Yet, she watched how he held the girl with one hand and poured two cups of water with the other. This child, a sure outlier for him. Something uncontrollable.

"Who is she?" Margot finally said. The girl had been staring at her.

Jason sucked his teeth. "After the quake, I saw her standing outside, under the statue. There was nobody with her. I went down to help, but no one came. I tried to take her to the police station, but they said they wouldn't be able to help her right away. The officer suggested I take her to social services. I tried to take her this morning, but—"

"Momma," the girl said. "Momma come. Momma gome home."

Margot looked down at the girl.

"At first she wouldn't say anything," Jason said. "I thought she was traumatized."

"What is she talking about?"

"I haven't been able to figure that out. It sounds like she thinks you're her mother."

Mother. The word made Margot shudder.

"She just sees a woman, and associates it with her mother," Knox said. "That's pretty obvious. And pardon me for playing devil's advocate, but I don't think she belongs here. You need to get her somewhere they can help her."

"You don't think I tried?" Jason said.

Margot saw Jason clench his fist behind his back. It was the first time he had even looked at Knox, and Margot saw the rage building, veins bulging in his neck as when they used to argue.

His face unfazed by the show of aggression, Knox said, "Maybe this was a bad idea, Margot. Looks like he's got his hands full."

She saw Jason turn red, his other hand placed atop the girl's shoulder, keeping her from walking over to Margot. The girl let out another series of sounds—not words but garbled animal noises. She tried to squirm free, but he wouldn't let go. She craned her neck, opened her mouth, and bit down on his hand.

Jason screeched, pulled his hand away.

The girl darted at Margot with arms open.

Margot flinched. Jason grabbed the girl, making her squeal louder.

"Can I please just have a minute alone with her?" Jason said. "Wait in here. I'll try to calm her." He picked her up and carried her into the other room.

Margot felt her blood pumping, throat closing, body temporarily frozen. A panic attack—such paralysis hadn't overcome her since losing the baby. At first, she didn't notice Knox holding her, his hand patting her hair softly.

"It's okay," he said. "Relax. Breathe. We can leave if you want to."

She shook her head, words having escaped her. "Need a minute," she said.

The girl's face, Margot thought—it looked much like her own, when she was a child. She wondered if Knox, or Jason, had noticed the resemblance. Weird coincidence, she thought, or maybe it's just my mind playing tricks on me. She hadn't eaten all day and couldn't remember the last time she had a drink of water.

And what about the girl's eyes?

Was Margot mistaken, or were they gray?

"Whatever you need," Knox said, his voice a whisper. "I'm here with you. Just say the word and we're gone. We don't need him. We'll find a way."

Of course, Knox would have been looking for any excuse to leave. The presence of the girl, not to mention her behavior, was his cue to abandon the whole Jason scenario. But Margot couldn't allow Knox's eagerness to sway her. She had to stand her ground. She wanted to tell him he was wrong, that they had nowhere else to go. Once they left Jason's, there would be no turning back; they'd have to find an encampment, like the ones outside the Hollywood Forever Cemetery or Silver Lake Reservoir.

"Maybe you should go check on Lane," she said.

Knox's jaw went slack. "And leave you alone up here?"

"I should try to talk to him by myself. The house has two stories. If he lets us stay, we don't even have to see him."

"And what about her?" he said, guiding her by the elbow out of earshot of Jason. "Don't you find it odd that he's got a kid here? I don't trust him. I know you two have a history, but a person can change a lot over a year."

She shook her arm from Knox's grip. "You don't have any reason not to trust him. You don't even know him."

He pursed his lips. "You sure you even want me to come back?"

Margot recognized the warning signs, a fight emerging.

"I want you to come back," she said. "Now's not the time to bicker. I need you on my team."

He turned to look out the kitchen window. "You're right," he said. "Sorry, I'm irritable. I probably need sleep. It's been a long couple of days."

"It's okay." In the light from the window, she saw the deep circles under his eyes. "Check on the dog and come right back. I'll ask him if he has any food. We both need to eat."

"Especially you," he said and caressed her stomach. "I'll be back in less than ten." She puckered her lips, leaned forward. He pressed his to hers and gave a slight smile. "We'll get through this. After what we've been through, we can make it through anything."

He nodded. "Right now, I just want to make it through a nap."

"Maybe when you get back." She wanted to take him to bed, shut the curtains, and sleep through the next week. She wanted a hot shower, a cup of coffee, an afternoon to paint and listen to Janis Joplin. Far removed from her list of wants was revisiting Jason and the house where they had dreamed of starting a family. She smiled for her husband, trying to hide her discomfort, her anxiety.

He squeezed her fingers, opened the door, and went outside. She closed it behind him, watched him descend the stairs until he was out of sight.

Alone in the kitchen, she felt unwelcomed, a guest in the home of a stranger. Though the creaks in the floor were familiar, the decorations on the walls her doing, somehow the house was unrecognizable. She thought of the saying about rivers, how you can never step into the same one twice. Here she was, in the house with Jason and a living child, an alternate version of the future she once envisioned.

She crossed to the living room. There, standing in the doorframe, she put her hand on the wall; she'd painted all of them egg white when they moved in. As she watched Jason settle the girl before a shelter of blankets, she dug a nail into the already-chipping paint.

Dear Margot,

Choices make us who we are.

And I choose not to hate you.

I choose not to loath or despise you.

I choose not to envy you.

How could I when I don't know the first thing about you?

How could I when I gave him enough reason to seek from someone else that which I could not give? Maybe, in a way, I should be thanking you for liberating the man I love. Without you, his life would have been one stuck in wait for a woman so consumed with her work that she could not reciprocate simple needs. You see, Margot—I pendulate back and forth. I try to be a forgiving person, but the truth is that resentment embitters me to the core. Because while I might try to let you and Knox off the hook, my transgressions being reason enough for him to stray, I can't forgive the act of betrayal when the act of honesty was always an option.

What defines a person's life, Margot? Achievements? Experiences? Or is it the sum of their actions? If our actions can be quantified, how, then, would we quantify betrayal? Certainly, the act of betrayal would not quantify gain; no, it would quantify subtraction—that is to say: it would lessen the sum of our defined life. That is to say: in choosing betrayal, you and Knox have lessened the sum of your lives.

But I can't wholeheartedly pin betrayal on you. For all I know he never told you about me. For all I know, you are innocent in the matter. But I can't believe that you weren't completely clueless. There must have come some point at which you asked him about his relationship status. And if that point in the conversation did not ever come to pass, there had to be some revelation to the fact that Knox's life was a shared one. I know he wouldn't betray me with someone so naive, so blind to the signs of another woman in his life. I refuse to believe that.

So, can you live with it, Margot?

Can you live with ruining someone's happiness?

Can you live with ruining me?

13

JASON SAT THE girl down on the floor in front of the fort. She fidgeted, trying to stand and sprint into the kitchen. What had come over her at the sight of Margot?

"You have to be good," he said, trying to sound stern without Margot hearing him. He looked at his hand. The perforated circle left by the girl's teeth had begun to swell. The skin was broken but not bleeding.

"If you bite me again, no more blueberries."

As if responding to the threat, the girl glowered at him. Just how much did she understand? She'd called Margot 'Momma'—after hours of showing little or no grasp of language. Sure, maybe Margot's husband had a point, but Jason suspected something deeper than merely associating a female with her mother. There were women outside the police station, and the girl mistook none of them for her mother.

He looked down at her; their eye contact felt stronger than choice, magnetic. The gray in her eyes shone, flickered again as they had at the cleft's edge. Her head pivoted, as did his, mirroring her. A sound—radio frequency?—buzzed somewhere in the house. He couldn't turn to locate its source, not with his gaze locked on the girl's. The static changed pitch, higher. Finally, a voice:

There is but a hairline...dividing life and death...All which exists...another form of that...which exists not...

The flicker in the girl's eyes faded back to a dull, ashen gray, her head upright again. Jason blinked, noticed sweat forming on his forehead. That sound, those words—had he imagined them, or—

"Jason, can we talk?"

He rose to see Margot standing in the doorway. Dizziness—from rising too fast? When he looked down, ready to stop the girl from running to Margot, he saw she'd disappeared into the fort.

"Knox is downstairs checking on our dog," Margot said.

He put his hands to his temples. "You hate dogs."

"I never said I hated them."

"I bet it was his before you came along. You must love this guy."

He'd suggested getting a dog twice: when they first moved to LA, and after losing the baby. Margot refused both times. The first time, her excuse was the responsibility. The second time, she looked at him with disdain and locked herself in the bathroom for an hour.

She looked at his hand. "You should put some peroxide on that."

"You're probably right." It occurred to him that the girl might be sick. Could that have caused her spell? Or had he hallucinated those words?

He told Margot he'd be right back and went into the bathroom. He found the medicine cabinet in disarray and a brown bottle of peroxide hidden behind a heap of junk under the sink. He opened the bottle, held his hand over the sink, and poured the cool liquid onto the bite mark, trying not to shriek as it bubbled.

"You should also put a bandage on it."

He nearly jumped at the sound of Margot's voice. She leaned against the doorframe, her eyes wandering, investigating the unchanged décor.

"Right. To prevent infection." With trembling hands, he searched for a box of Band-Aids. Was it the pain, or was it his proximity to her?

"Looks like you need some help."

She reached below him and dug through the under-the-sink junk. As she emerged with gauze and a bandage wrap, he got a whiff of her hair, a hint of grease and sugarplum. He inched nearer to breathe her in, almost close enough to touch.

"I honestly didn't expect to see you. Ever again."

He couldn't look at her for longer than a few seconds while she spun the gauze around his hand. Was her evasion of direct contact intentional?

She fastened the aluminum clips to the bandage.

"We had nowhere else to go," she said.

Jason wanted to ask, And how is that my problem?

Instead, he asked, "He doesn't have any friends? What about family?"

She returned the peroxide and remaining bandage wrap to the space beneath the sink.

"Not in the city," she said.

Jason knew the feeling. When they first moved to LA they had struggled to make friends. Those they did make were tenuous at best. There had been a few from their respective jobs, people to share overpriced drinks with after work. They never amounted to more than acquaintances.

"He moved here around the same time we did," she said. "With his ex."

"I heard about what happened to her," he said, biting his lip. No matter how much he wanted to hate Margot's husband, nobody deserved to lose someone like that. After the miscarriage, he and Margot had tried therapy—he'd suggested it after she expressed having thoughts of self-harm. It was natural, the therapist had assured them, for both women and men to experience postpartum depression. Suicidal thoughts, however, generally occurred in only severe cases. Or so they'd been told. He couldn't imagine how Knox dealt with it all this time.

Margot crossed her arms, stiffened her shoulders.

"How'd you hear about it?" she asked.

"Dave and Randiah," he said. "I haven't talked to them for months, though."

He'd met Dave at work, and Margot and Randiah were friendly enough at their first double date to make hangouts a regular thing.

"Neither have I," she said. "I got the impression they thought I was some kind of whore."

Jason coughed on his saliva. "Nobody thought that," he stammered. "Nobody would ever think that about you." He put his hand on her shoulder and squeezed. She eyed his hand, her face tight as if having sucked a lemon. "Sorry. I didn't—"

"It's okay. Really."

And with that infinitesimal moment of contact, the chains of restraint binding Jason came undone.

"We could have gotten through the loss together," he said. "I know I pressured you to try again. You weren't ready. I'm sorry. But losing you was worse than anything, Margot."

Her jaw jutted.

"It wasn't just what we lost," she said through her teeth. "I felt stifled. Pressured, yes. To try again, but also before that. It wasn't exactly my decision to move here." She closed her eyes, craned her neck. "I needed to take control. Of my body, my life, my decisions. It doesn't excuse what I did. I've made mistakes, I know that. But the point is that they were mine to make."

Jason felt the air leave him, and just as he opened his mouth to speak a noise came from the kitchen—the back door opening, closing.

"Knox," Margot said and left the bathroom.

Beyond the door, Jason saw the fort's entrance flap rustling. For the first time since finding the girl, he'd forgotten about her.

"Weird," Margot said, returning. "I could've sworn I heard the door."

Jason rushed to the fort. Down on his knees, he poked his head in.

The girl was gone.

"Shit," he said. "She left."

He ran past Margot and out the door. Outside, he scanned the area and saw only an empty yard, empty streets. He put his hands on both guardrails, hoisted himself up and over them, and landed with a smack on the concrete. Numbness in his legs, he stumbled through the yard until he could run again, toward the only place he knew the girl would go.

Amazing how all it takes is one scientific or technological advancement to change everything.

The letterpress.

The automobile.

The computer.

It appears that someone from CERN caught wind of my recent failures with RIFT and requested the data from Tajū. Had I known about this request, I would have certainly denied Tajū access to my files. This goes to show how counterproductive my intuitions are because CERN was taken aback.

With my attempts to accelerate a reionizer with a copper core, it was discovered that the carbine reactor started to emit a pale-yellow light. This light is precisely what CERN wanted to question. Tajū provided them with a detailed schematic of the reionizer and the copper core, which led CERN to give the pale light a closer investigation. Their tests revealed that the pale light was a blanket of what had been a previously unknown sub-atomic particle now called the Boson Rift Neutrino Particle, or the Spirit Particle for short.

It turns out that these Spirit Particles are the first known inverse of dark matter.

Tajū doesn't exactly know what this means for our collider, but he has told me that it changes our primary trajectory. He once said that our work could change the world.

But now he's saying that our work will change history.

I think he means this literally.

Late night—

I can't help thinking about her. Logged into his Facebook and re-read their messages. The message log has grown since I last read it. I went to her profile from his page. Turns out she's with someone, too. Someone named Jason.

No shame, it seems.

But her profile only told me so much. Where she's from (Florida). What she does (teacher). Turns out she's a painter. And I hate to say it—a decent one. Makes sense for K. to be attracted to someone who makes art versus someone who is a slave to science.

But I'm not a slave.

It's my choice.

My calling.

I could leave this place now if that is what I truly desired. I could find this Margot and confront her. I could demand an explanation from K. I could reveal that I'm late; I could propose having it without him. I could choose to stop loving him.

I could, I could, I could.

But there are some things I simply cannot do even though my will burns hot.

I need sleep.

Need to relieve my mind of this.

Can't afford another mistake.

14

Crossing the Roundabout, Knox craved a cigarette. His heart pounded so hard he thought Lane would hear it when he opened the door to the Jeep. The dog had seen him coming, snout to the crack of the window, tail wagging.

"At least someone's glad to see me." He hooked the leash to Lane's collar and guided him to the street. While the dog sniffed for a spot to pee, Knox took slow, deep breaths to stabilize his pulse. He had never felt such jealousy with Tiffany. When they first started dating, there had been no one from her recent past for him to contend with, no lingering loves or loose ends. She pledged total devotion to him, saying she'd never felt quite so sure about anyone. At first, Tiffany's approbations had amused and warmed him, but after her death, he wondered to what extent her love might have been an obsession. It had only been in light of her absence that her history of narcissistic behavior took shape in his mind.

Exaggerated feelings of self-importance, especially regarding her latest project. Excessive need for admiration, which drained Knox whenever they had time together. What had disturbed him most, though, was the way she cleverly masked her lack of empathy; any time he'd shown reservations about their relationship—whether moving to LA or having children someday—she exploited her love for him, her unthwarted belief that they were destined to be together, as superior to his fragile convictions.

"I would give my life for you," she'd told him in bed the night she learned about her job opportunity on the West Coast. "And you're not even willing to entertain a change of location, even though your career opportunities would abound there."

The therapist was the one to educate him about the textbook indicators of Tiffany's pathologies, but he still found it troublesome to pin blame on someone simply because some manual claimed to classify them.

People weren't so cut and dried. For example, he never pegged himself as someone who'd end up unfaithful.

Though his time with Tiffany surpassed his with Margot, the need to be with Margot had been far greater than with Tiffany. A force beyond his control, notwithstanding his wavering feelings for Tiffany in the wake of her growing distance and increasingly attached disposition.

He glanced back at Jason's house. Was it foolish of Knox to reject the prospect of safety, of protecting his wife, even if the most immediate source of shelter was her ex? Of course it was. For better or worse, he'd promised. In good times and bad.

Lane barked. When Knox turned his head, he saw something running toward the beach—an animal? No, a person—a small one—the girl from inside Jason's house.

"Hey!"

He looked around for Margot or Jason but saw no one, not even a passerby.

Lane tugged on the leash, pulling and nearly tripping Knox. Where was she going, and at such speed? He gave in to the dog's force and started to run, the girl yards ahead of them. He called after her again, but she kept up her pace, not once looking back. As they passed the storefronts leading to the boardwalk, Lane burst forward, and the leash slipped from Knox's grip. He staggered, trying to reclaim it from the ground, and tripped over a concrete slab in the process. When he looked up, he saw the girl running through the sand, Lane close behind. What reason did the dog have to chase the girl? Lane hadn't been near her, hadn't before picked up her scent. He briefly worried the dog might attack her, despite his gentle history. Knox had never seen him pursue anything—animal, mineral, or vegetable—with such urgency.

"Lane! Here, boy!"

Lane stopped, but not to heed Knox. The dog kept its distance from the girl, barking wildly at something else. From the boardwalk, Knox saw the colossal hole in the earth, the size of half a football field, or a limestone quarry from back home, before rain and spring waters rushed in to fill it. The crater obscured the beach's harmony. Where smooth sand had lined the shore, jagged rock forms now bulged. He couldn't believe it was a result of the quake. He'd not heard of seismic activity powerful enough in this region to disfigure the land so drastically. Then, a jolted memory of an email from Tiffany. Something about her project and its potential for such damage.

Knox saw the girl take a step closer to the edge of the crater, looking down into the hole. He plodded cautiously through the sand, past Lane, still barking, scared that any sudden movements would startle the girl. What had put the dog into a frenzy, if not the girl? Over the barking, he heard something from the boardwalk, voices calling his name. He looked back and saw Jason running toward them, Margot hard on his heels.

"Stop her!" Jason called. "Get her away from there!"

Knox spun around and sprinted. The girl turned her head. Her hair flailed in the wind. He raced toward her until his fingers were within an inch of the fabric of the back of her shirt. Then she leaned forward and fell into the cavity.

Tuesday—

Things are evolving rather quickly.

The Spirit Particles have thrown the proverbial wrench into my research.

And put me at an ethical crossroads.

As it turns out, when dark matter is manipulated on a subatomic level, a rift is certainly possible. We have learned that with a new black hole created, there is an additional rift which, in line with superstring theory, creates an additional ten dimensions. But now that we're learning more about the Spirit Particles, it seems we're also learning more about what's on the other side of a black hole.

Dark matter, like regular matter, is never-ending. There is no beginning; there is no end. It is neither Alpha nor Omega. Like the ouroboros. It simply exists in a continuum. Time also works this way. This is to say that the possibility of both future and past is eliminated. Time can also be thought of as the ouroboros. It is wrong to think of a timeline as one line with a beginning and an end. It is wrong to think of time in terms of history. Time is on an endless loop, spinning and spinning. A snake eating its tail.

But the snake has its makeup. It is one whole snake.

However, superstring theory tells us there is more than one dimension to the snake.

And the creation of black holes creates even more snakes.

Multiple timelines.

Multiple universes.

And they all exist simultaneously.

When a new one is created, it turns out that Spirit Particles determine the laws of each snake, which I will henceforth refer to as Coils.[∞]

Each Coil exists in tandem with the other Coils.

[∞] The Spirit Particles couple with DNA. In fact, DNA is needed for there to be a microcosm on the other side of the rift. And maybe the only way to reclaim what was mine is to obtain DNA that will create a new Coil made from the same elements. I don't know how it will unfold. But at this point, what do I have to lose by trying?

The constants are the same.[∞] *Ex: Each snake is still a snake. It would not be true to say that each snake is a turtle. Instead of a pillar of turtles going all the way down through infinity, it is more precise to envision an endless table of snakes eating their own tails.*

[∞] This is to say: if one Coil is comprised of the constants A, B, C, and D, then every subsequent Coil will be comprised of some variation of A, B, C, and D. Let Coil I represent A, B, C, and D; let Coil II represent A, C, D, and B; let Coil III represent A, D, C, B; Let Coil IV represent A, B, D, C. With this combination of variables, there are twenty-four permutations. The constants, however, remain the same. Consider all of the possible variables in any given combination and you will find infinite permutations.

15

KNOX LANDED ON his chest with his arms outstretched over the crater's lip, feeling the cold air between his fingers, the hardness of rock under his palms. Down below, in the hole, he saw only darkness. No sign of the girl, no sound of an object—someone—falling. He peered into the darkness. Mesmerized, Knox reached further into the abyss, his body inching over the edge. A light, violet, within arm's reach, yet impossibly far away.

He felt tugging at his ankles, pulling him from the light. He tried to grab hold of rock, digging his fingernails into stone, suddenly desperate to make contact with the violet light, warm and inviting. Unable to keep his place, the force behind him won. Sunrays pierced his eyes. Total white.

"Knox," said a voice. Above him, coming into focus—Margot.

"What happened?" He considered, briefly, that the bright lights were those of a hospital room. As reality set in, along with the void feeling of waking from a deep sleep, he remembered the girl. His stomach turned.

Next to him, on his hands and knees, bent over the side of the crevice, was Jason.

"I have to go in," he said. "I have to find her, go in after her."

"No, you don't," Margot said, yanking him away from the brink by his shirt collar. Knox heard Lane's yelps, the dog at his feet, nuzzling them with his snout. He lifted himself onto his elbows. He felt too weak to go any higher. Did he pass out, faint? What had drained him of his energy?

The violet light, he thought—fragments of it remained in the back of his mind, when he closed his eyes, still burning in his retinas.

And the girl, what about her? Surely the gorge had a bottom. The question was how far down it went. He couldn't believe it, but he felt himself siding with Jason, the urge to follow the girl, to allow the darkness to encompass him, growing stronger.

"Maybe he's right," Knox said. "I think we have to go in after her."

"Are you crazy? We all know what happened to her." Margot started to step toward the edge, but Jason grabbed her ankle.

"Don't look. One of us has to not look."

"What do you mean?"

Jason turned to Knox. "You felt it," he said. "I know you did. Like something calling you." He released Margot, her feet close enough for her to jump down into the hole.

"I don't know what you're talking about. You both sound nuts."

"He's right," Knox said. "I felt something. Listen to him, Margot."

She put the back of her hand to his forehead. "Doesn't feel like a fever, but I'm worried about you." Knox swatted her hand away. He hated this feeling—wanting to probe

Jason for his thoughts. He forced himself to meet Jason's gaze and tilted his head, urging him to explain.

"Before you two came," Jason started, "I was walking her to social services. There was a crowd of people here, taking pictures. Next thing, I hear people screaming. Someone, maybe a few people, must have fallen in. They all started running, and the girl—she starts running toward it when everyone else is running away. I nearly lost her. Before that, when I found her, I thought she was deaf and dumb or something. Then she starts saying the words, 'Go home,' over and over. It was the only thing she said, other than calling you 'Momma.'" With his hand blocking the sun, he looked up at Margot. "Then she ran over here like it was calling to her. She'd have jumped in if I didn't grab her, and even then, she fought me. It was then I looked down, into the hole, and I saw it."

"The violet light," said Knox.

Jason nodded. "I couldn't look away. Something came over me, like the kid. I wanted to go in, I didn't care if that meant the end. I had to snap myself out of it."

"I have to see what you guys are talking about," Margot said, brushing past them.

"No, Margot—!"

Knox tackled her around her hips and pinned her to the ground.

"What the hell's gotten into you?" she said. Knox tightened his grip as she tried to wrestle free. "Let me go, Knox." The veins bulged in her neck. "A little girl just died."

"I don't think she's dead," Jason said. "After Knox went outside, the way she looked at me. Her eyes…they were…"

"Gray," Margot said.

"I've never seen anything like it," Jason said. "Have you?"

Margot shook her head.

"I thought maybe she was sick. But after she bit me, I saw the change in her eyes, then I heard a voice. It was like bad reception on a radio, but then there were these broken sentences, as clear in my head as actual speech. 'There is but a hairline dividing life and death.'"

Knox shuddered, felt Margot's eyes on him.

"She said this to you?" she asked.

Jason shrugged. "Not exactly. I know I sound crazy, but I don't think she said it. It felt more like she thought it."

Knox's limbs had gone limp. He released Margot, reeling from the last bit of Jason's story.

Margot stood, wiped the sand from her pants. "I'm going back to the house," she said. "I'm going to be sick. I can't deal with this right now."

Knox watched as she turned away and started back toward the boardwalk.

A memory of Tiffany's handwriting came to him.

This is not goodbye.

He swallowed hard. "I've heard that before," he said.

Lane mewled and licked Knox's cheek. He pushed the dog aside, trying to remember the rest of the words from Tiffany's departing note.

It is always possible for things to get worse.

The universe can throw curveballs, even those of the reality-changing variety.

As it turns out, Tajū has sold CERN *the rights to the code I wrote that created the Spirit Particles.* CERN *has patented the code, which will stop any further use of our particle collider.*

Which puts me out of a job.

Which rips my life's work right out of my hands.

Tajū technically owned all the work I did since it was completed in his laboratory. It was never really mine to begin with.

I asked Tajū why he would do this when we had all worked so hard.

He couldn't give me an answer, but I can only assume it was because CERN *offered him a price he couldn't refuse.*

I have been given twenty-four hours to vacate the lab.

But I have nowhere to go.

All the other employees have left, so I'm here.

By myself.

I need an escape.

I need a way out of this.

16

Margot entered the house, still unlocked from when Jason rushed out looking for the girl, and ran straight for the bathroom. At the toilet, she buckled to her knees and held her head over the seat. Bile rose and she spat it out, keeping her hair out of the way. What was there in her stomach to throw up? The green-yellow liquid swirled in the bowl, barely enough to warrant the gagging that followed.

She wiped her lip, stood, and went to the kitchen. The waters Jason had poured earlier still sat on the counter. She lifted one glass, chugged it, the water cool and fresh as it gushed down her throat. She repeated with the second glass and, once emptied, put her back to the counter and slid down to the floor. The house was quiet without the men and the girl. It was the first time she'd been alone in the house since the day she had left Jason. She closed her eyes and listened, the intensity of the silence heightened by the lack of electricity—no appliances, no creaks in the walls from other neighbors like back at The Libra.

The Libra, she thought—were those people still occupying their home? And since it had been invaded, was it even their home? Her stomach gurgled. She needed to find food, if not for her then for the baby. From her spot on the floor, she reached to the refrigerator door, cracked it open.

A stench seeped out—rotted food—and she closed the door again. She pulled herself up and looked through the cabinets, finding a sleeve of saltines and a can of beef stew. Thank God the stove is gas-powered, she thought, and searched for a pot while chewing a stale cracker.

She found what was left of Jason's cookware in the dishwasher where it must have been since before the blackout. While heating the stew she thought about what Jason had said, how he'd heard voices in his head. She probably would have thought him insane if it wasn't for the words he iterated: *There is but a hairline dividing life and death.* Although Knox hadn't read the note as many times as she had, Margot knew that he recognized the words, too.

She ate the stew from the pot while sitting at the table she and Jason had picked up from IKEA. Tiffany's note was still in the Jeep, tucked deep into one of the bags she'd packed. With the last bite of potato in her mouth she stood and went outside, hoping to get to her bag before Knox or Jason returned.

The streets still empty, Margot ran to the Jeep and opened the hatchback. She reached into her bag and tossed her clothes aside until she found the note. Once unfolded, the words etched in Tiffany's handwriting struck Margot as part of an artifact that should have been long destroyed. She put the paper to her nose—its scent, an earthy chypre, still Tiffany's, one Margot would have never worn. Her eyes focused on the words.

Would you again Eurydice receive, should fate her quick-spun thread of life re-weave?

Engrossed in the note, Margot lingered on the sentences. There's no way Jason could have known, she thought. No way for him to make up the exact string of words.

For me, there was no other method; the noose, or as Virgil put it, the coil of unbecoming death, is the purest way to do it—reliant entirely on mass...

There is but a hairline dividing life and death...

Would you again Eurydice receive, should fate her quick-spun thread of life re-weave?

Margot had only read of Orpheus in a college Lit class. She remembered the story of the legendary musician and poet, braving a journey into the land of the dead to resurrect his bride, Eurydice, who had just died from a snakebite. After Orpheus's petition to Hades and Persephone, Persephone—the Goddess of the underworld—allowed him and Eurydice to return under one condition:

Orpheus would lead his wife out of the underworld.

But he was to never look back.

Not until they had returned to the land of the living.

As Margot scanned the note, she thought about the conversations she and Knox had had about Tiffany—her career in quantum physics, their years together before moving to LA, but never about this myth.

And only once outside of the note had Margot heard of Tiffany's experiment—RIFT. She scanned the line in the note, *If RIFT succeeds, maybe my life's work won't have been for nothing; but if it fails, then what purpose will my countless hours of research and experiments have served?* What purpose was RIFT supposed to serve? When Margot had brought it up to Knox, he shut the conversation down by leaving the apartment without a word. She'd figured it was too painful for him to talk about, that it was best left with the parts of the past they'd agreed to no longer speak of.

Margot had researched Tiffany online and learned she was some kind of genius, given grants for her innovative research. Margot had often felt like she would never compare in Knox's eyes, that her paintings and career as an educator were insubstantial in light of what Tiffany had done with her life. The therapist had urged her to never compare herself to other people, but Margot couldn't keep the jealousy at bay. Knowing of Tiffany's accomplishments only made Margot strive to paint more, seek out her own grants, prove to herself and Knox that she, too, was destined for greatness.

As if her life wasn't enough—one thing Margot had that Tiffany didn't. Countless times Knox had made her promise to never resort to such measures, no matter how bad things seemed. She understood how a person could feel so hopeless, especially after losing something into which so much love was invested. But Tiffany's note, laced with random letters, was personal—not just at Knox, but also at Margot. Margot didn't want to believe Tiffany had intended for her death to double as an act of revenge. With all of Tiffany's talent and ingenuity, it wouldn't have surprised Margot if she'd somehow orchestrated the blackout and the events that followed.

That's sick, Margot thought. Who am I to blame the dead?

She closed her eyes, listened to the soft breeze drifting by.

But death doesn't wash clean the horrific, vindictive, or manipulative actions done in life. No, she couldn't let Tiffany off that easily. Margot thought back to Knox's bouts of screaming, a gutting reaction to his pain, rage, and guilt. Panic attacks, surely. Deep trauma. How dare Tiffany inflict that upon him? And for what? Infidelity? Unfaithful he may have been, but in the year Margot had been married to Knox, she'd known him as nothing other than devout, tender, urbane, ardent. Their time together was but a scratch to the wound that had become Tiffany and Knox's relationship, Margot was well aware—but isn't a year long enough to get a sense of the core of a person?

She had half a mind to finally get rid of Tiffany's note. It was all Margot could do to keep from tearing it up and letting the shreds float away in the wind.

She'd have done it if she didn't believe the note contained the key to understanding the pit into which the little girl had disappeared.

It's only natural to question what happens to us after we die.

So many people cling to the hope of heaven. And what a beautiful hope it is. To think that we will be born again in a new place, a new world, with all our sins forgiven.

But not everyone can accept that. Some can barely wrap their heads around God at all.

Others are so afraid of life after death they have built entire spiritual beliefs around making the cycle of life cease.

They call it Nirvana.

I am more prone to believing that matter is neither created nor destroyed.

But I'm not so quick to get in line with the Buddhists, either.

As a scientist, it is nearly impossible for me to suspend my disbelief and see beyond life on an atomic level. I know that atoms are in our bodies forever until they become carbon dioxide. Until we are food for future organisms. There is calcium and phosphorous in our bones that become part of plant life. There is helium within us that, upon death, defies gravity and drifts into outer space.

But now we have the Spirit Particles.

And perhaps a new way to think about life after death.

17

"You probably think I'm crazy," Jason said, watching Margot disappear behind buildings along the boardwalk. He'd grown tired of chasing after Margot, even if introspectively. Tired of expecting her to do anything other than run. Besides, it was Knox's job to follow her now.

"That's not what I think," Knox said. "Honestly, I don't know what I think. I know I saw the kid jump in, and I know what I felt. Something got into me, like I was possessed. So, if you're crazy, then I guess that makes me crazy, too."

"How can we both be crazy if we experienced the same thing?"

Knox shrugged. "Those words you heard—the ones in your head. I know where I heard them before. When Margot and I got together, I was with someone else. When she found out about Margot, she didn't take it too well. She—"

"I know what happened," Jason said. He wanted to spare them of the details.

Knox glared, quizzical. "Well, she left a note. The words you said you heard—they were in the note, practically verbatim."

Jason shivered. He asked, "It's got to be a coincidence, right?" though he doubted the very question.

Knox tipped his head toward the hole in the ground then gestured back at the city.

"Do you believe any of this is coincidence?"

Jason shook his head, stared down at the sand. "I stopped believing in that a while ago."

"I don't know how to tell you this," Knox said before clearing his throat. "Margot's pregnant."

Jason's jaw went tight, teeth clenched. "I didn't realize," he said. He thought of the bathroom, of wanting to kiss her as she dressed his wound. Of her explaining all the other reasons for leaving. Why hadn't she told him then? Why did he have to hear it from her husband?

"I know it must be hard," Knox went on. "She told me about what happened with you two."

"You don't know the first thing about it," Jason snapped.

He looked up at Knox, who had recoiled, holding his dog.

Softening, Jason continued, "I know it's not your fault. We wouldn't have lasted whether she met you or not."

"I just thought you had a right to know."

Jason nodded. "You should go after her."

"What about you?"

"You know what I'm going to do." He turned toward the chasm, just enough to remind himself how inviting its darkness had been earlier that day.

He wondered, at this point, after the last year, what was left—if anything—in his life to forsake.

And, thinking of the child who had mysteriously appeared before him, what there was to salvage.

"Do you think that is the best idea?" Knox asked.

"We both felt it," Jason said. "I'm going after the kid."

"Margot's right. She could be dead."

"I don't think she is. And I don't think you think she is, either."

"I'll wait here," Knox said. "What if you don't come back? What if you need help getting her out? We could get a rope, or—"

"There's no point," Jason said. "Go to Margot. Keep the house locked until I come back."

"You don't have to—"

"Go," Jason said, kicking dirt at Knox and the dog. Knox stood, leered at Jason, and started walking. Jason watched as he and the dog trekked through the sand, both looking back at him, hesitant. He waved them on, presenting an illusion of confidence.

He waited until they were out of view. Once they disappeared, he reached his hand into the darkness, the violet light untouchable, no matter how far he stretched his arm. All he felt was cold air against his fingers, gritty sand beneath his knees. He called into the cavern but heard nothing save the echo of his voice. He recalled seeing the girl jump in, the seconds before Knox tried to save her. Her face had been so determined, fearless. The only time he remembered her panicking was when he prevented her from jumping in—so what did he have to be afraid of?

Maybe if Margot and Knox had never shown up, he would have been more tentative. But now, he thought, she's pregnant. Any chance we had is gone. He wondered if she still cared about the family they almost had, or if the thought had been erased when she left him.

He drew a breath, remembered the girl's at-first incomprehensible words:

Home.

Go home.

He closed his eyes, saw Margot's face and the girl's, and dove over the edge.

18

KNOX WANTED TO turn around and stop Jason, convince him to come back to the house and think everything through. But at the same time, Jason choosing self-destruction was not Knox's cross to bear. He needed to get back to Margot, despite the remnants of Tiffany haunting him.

His thoughts stirred: How did Jason know about Tiffany? Would he have been so willing to go after the girl if Knox hadn't told him about Margot's pregnancy? Margot—how was he to take care of her, and their child, without a doctor or proper health care? As he turned the corner, he saw her at the Jeep, reading intently from a piece of paper. Lane looked up, head cocked, seeking his permission before running over to her.

"Go ahead, boy," he said, and the dog trotted ahead without him.

The note, Knox realized—she's reading Tiffany's note.

He saw Lane startle her. She glanced up, saw Knox coming, and hid the note from view.

"I thought you burned that," he called from across the roundabout.

She opened her mouth, revealed the note, and shrugged. "I couldn't," she said.

"Let me see it." He reached for it, but she retracted.

"I don't think that's a good idea," she said and looked behind Knox. "Where's Jason?"

He couldn't retain eye contact with her.

"He went in," he said. "To look for the girl."

He'd stunned her.

She did a double take, asked, "Are you serious?" and went to run, but Knox held out his hand.

"We should go inside the house," he pleaded. "That's what he wanted us to do."

He saw the tears forming in her eyes, her gaze locked on the road leading to the boardwalk, the sun hovering over the horizon. Lane walked between them, and Knox saw him licking at Margot's ankles.

"Something's not right," she said. "I don't know what's real anymore." She walked past him, toward the house.

He followed her, Lane close behind, until they were upstairs. He closed the kitchen door and sat at the table, watching Margot pace back and forth.

"We need to talk about this," she said, staring at the note.

He put his hands under the table and pinched himself so hard he thought the skin would break. As if trying to solve the mystery of Tiffany would miraculously converge the fault lines fracturing their relationship. He exhaled a defiant breath, said, "Sure."

Her neck tensed, and she neutralized her face. "Is there even the slightest possibility she had something to do with all of this?"

Knox fought the urge to pinch himself again.

He thought back to the string of emails Tiffany had started to send him, and how they abruptly stopped. Right around the time he met Margot. He wished he could access his inbox, but then he looked to the folded papers in Margot's hands. Tiffany hadn't stopped writing him letters. She'd just stopped sending them.

"It's possible," he said.

"Tell me what you know about her work," Margot said. "Her project, RIFT. How could she possibly have caused the blackout? The hole in the ground?"

He turned his face away, closed his eyes, and caught his leg jittering up and down.

"I don't know as much as you might think. I know she studied black holes, the effects of gravity. Toward the end, a few weeks before you and I—" He bit his lower lip, took a breath. "Her lab had given her permission to purchase some equipment. I couldn't tell you much about it, other than she was excited. She'd written some code. I think the goal was to recreate a black hole, or at least a model of one that could exist here, on Earth."

When he opened his eyes, he saw her placing the note in front of him on the table. "What do you think she means at the end? About atoms being in our bodies, our bones becoming part of plant life?"

He found the section and traced his finger over the words.

"I think she wasn't in a good state of mind when she wrote this," he said.

"You knew her better than anyone, Knox. These aren't typically things you would find in a suicide note."

He cringed, put his hands over his ears. He felt like a child trying to block out the world.

"Please," she said.

He faced her, his heart beating so fast it made his vision blurry. "She had some kind of infatuation with the afterlife. Sometimes, after work, we'd have a drink and she'd start talking about what happens when we die, about dark matter. And then, their recent discovery. Spirit particles. She thought black holes were more than just things in outer space, that they were some kind of doorway to the other side."

He was reminded, more so with over a year's distance from Tiffany, how unreal her lectures had sounded.

"And what did you think whenever she talked about this stuff?"

He looked down at the note, focused on the words *Awaiting the beginning of infinity.*

"She was too involved with her work and too close to her project. Maybe a little overzealous, but I tried to be supportive. But the fact is, she was pathological. She had a way of blinding me from the truth with her delusions of grandiosity."

He looked up from the note to find Margot's eyebrow raised.

"But did you believe her? Did you think any of her ideas had merit, or did you think they were all bogus?"

Knox surveyed the kitchen, wondering if Jason had cigarettes or liquor lying around. "Tiffany wasn't stupid," he said. "A textbook narcissist? Yes, but she was very intelligent. Her ideas couldn't have been completely bunk."

He couldn't help getting up and searching the cupboards and cabinets, overpowered by the urge to smoke and drink.

"We need to reevaluate what she wrote," Margot said. "It could be the key. We have to try to decipher it, and I need to go back to the beach and look inside that hole myself."

Mention of the crater brought back the veil of hypnosis Knox had felt at its mouth, and he slammed one of the cabinet doors shut. "I don't want to hear any more about it," he said, afraid to turn and face Margot. "I'm going to be sick."

He jumped when he felt her hands on his shoulders, his muscles tense, trembling.

"Come with me," she said, massaging his arms and neck.

He nodded and followed her to the living room. She guided him to the couch, sat him down, and nestled into his arms. As awkward as it felt to lie across Jason's furniture, Margot's warmth was enough to make him drowsy, his eyes already half-closed.

"I don't know what to do," he said. "I'm torn. Powerless. Can barely think straight."

"Remember what you said before? We're not powerless. We just need a little rest."

"All I need is an hour or two," he said.

"I'll set the alarm on my phone," she said and poked his belly.

He put his lips on her forehead, shut his eyelids. He felt the onset of a dream, his mind racing with thoughts of Jason and the crater, and he imagined himself stuck until the end of time at the bottom of a dark, sulfurous well.

There is a way out, and there are many tools to consider for the execution.[∞]

But no method is either quick or painless.

One thing I am certain of: I will need to set the collider to full power. I will need every bit of output it can handle to create the rift.

I've been wrestling with the possible outcomes.

Consequences.

During my initial tests, a run using only a fraction of the collider's output created a small earthquake.

I'm afraid to think of what might happen as a result.

Our tests average between magnitudes of four-point-seven and five. Tajū swears we could achieve

[∞] My search history, read by any sane person at the moment, would clearly appear as a cry for help. However, there are no sane people around to read my search history. There are no people around at all. No one with whom to discuss the most painless way to remove oneself. But even that conversation would be a joke, the punch line being that energy is neither created nor destroyed.

seven. A quake that strong would cause blackouts and far worse. Tajū informed me of how it took engineers over a week to fully restore power for millions of people after the magnitude six-point-seven hit Hokkaido, Japan in 2018. He didn't need me to remind him of the six-point-seven here in Northridge in 1994.

Could LA survive an outage of greater scale? ∞

My objective is not to cause so much destruction.

Just enough.

But if I'm already gone, will it even matter?

There will be multiple universes in which the city is fine.

Something like this was bound to happen to Los Angeles eventually.

When the Large Hadron Collider announced the capabilities of creating black holes, the media branded it as a doomsday device that would devour Earth in its entirety.

Surely, I can't be the sole person to blame.

What I'm not sure of: will I have the willpower to witness what I've caused?

∞ Not long ago, there was an explosion at the Northridge power plant that caused one hundred and forty thousand people to lose power in the San Fernando Valley. Even this was inconsequential compared to the destruction seen in '94.

I could probably stand the guilt of LA resting on my shoulders.

But not the whole planet.

I can choose the coordinates of the event horizon. I can choose the time the collider will produce the rift.

No matter what I do, once I set the collider to produce, there is no turning back.

With the addition of Tajū's Radial Fermion Expander, it will take one year at the least. I suppose there is no time to waste. The entire collider would have to be destroyed to prevent the rift from being produced. Considering the amount of money, time, and work that was put into creating it, I can't foresee its destruction anytime soon.

But waiting three hundred sixty-five days for the event horizon is not an option for me. I'm not brave enough to face those days. Those nights. Am I brave enough to face you?

If I set the coordinates and the time of production before I leave this lab tonight, I will have to live with what I've done for the next year. An additional code I've written will make the collider appear dormant to anyone at the lab, and I've made it impossible to reverse the ignition.

I know I can never turn back, but I'm afraid if I do not do it tonight, I will never have another chance.

19

MARGOT OPENED HER eyes and saw Knox asleep. She rose from the couch slowly and, with her eyes still heavy, looked around the living room. She half-expected Jason to be sitting on the adjacent chair or for the girl to poke her head out of the fort's entryway. But the house was empty, silent. The sun had already set, the moon visible through the window, its light resting upon Knox's calm face. How long had they been out? The thought of Jason back at the beach almost sent her running toward the door. However, she knew there was no hope. If he'd already gone into the crater, then it was history. There would be no bringing him or the girl back. The urge to vomit again crept into her body and she went into the bathroom, held her head over the toilet, and dry heaved. When nothing came out, she looked to see if she'd woken Knox, but his snores let her know he wouldn't be waking up any time soon.

She paced around the house, snooping through Jason's things. His bedroom—their old bedroom—was more immaculate than ever. It looked like a photo from a Williams-Sonoma catalog. Her messiness had so often counterbalanced his obsessive tidiness, but now there was nothing with which Jason's controlling tendencies had to contend. Running her hand along the comforter they'd brought from Florida, she recalled a dream she'd had on the couch while in Knox's arms: the house, full of love and life—though not with Knox, but with Jason. They had a child together. They'd never lost their baby. She'd envisioned them on the ground, rolling around, wrapped up so tightly they may as well have been a single organism.

Now fully awake, the dream was so distant it was hard to believe she had conjured it only moments ago. It was hard for her to imagine Jason sleeping alone in their bed all the nights she'd been away. She wished she could even pretend he'd been with at least one other woman since then, but she knew it wasn't true.

She stubbed her toe on the way to the kitchen, the house completely dark except for the dim moonlight. She'd cursed loudly but Knox didn't budge, his snores reaching chainsaw levels. Her stomach rumbled, and she noticed a container of oats in the kitchen. Her baby was growing—or at least trying to—and there was barely anything she could do to ensure its proper care and nutrition. She boiled water for the oats and sat on the cold kitchen floor, running her hands along its smooth surface. How long had it been since she'd last prayed? She could not remember, the practice as far and strange as the dream she'd left behind on the couch. She wanted to blame God for putting her there, trapping her in a city without electricity or means of escape. She wanted to blame God for taking one child and giving her another, but she knew she was the one to blame. So many others she could have tried to blame—Tiffany, Jason, Knox. But she was just as culpable as all of them.

Soon Knox's snoring silenced, and Margot ate a bowl of oatmeal on the kitchen floor, the light of the moon cast upon her, her eyes fixed out the door's window. She thought about whether or not the invaders were still at The Libra, whether she would ever return to that building again. She thought about all the people without homes before the outage, and the newly homeless. How fortunate she and Knox were to be in Jason's house, that Jason hadn't left LA.

Jason—she couldn't believe Knox had left him behind. But what was he to do? It wasn't her place to blame Knox, especially if Jason had made the decision himself. But it was clear he wasn't in his right mind. And that girl—Margot recalled her dream, remembered that she'd seen the girl, and, in the dream, the girl with the gray eyes was their daughter. She shuddered and got to her feet. There were only a few options left, given the circumstances. She and Knox could wait out the next few days in the house, during which Knox would search for food. That was probably the smartest option. They could leave the house, risking the impending dangers of the city, hoping to find another way out.

Or she could wait until the first rays of sunlight and return to the beach, look inside the gorge as she should have when the girl jumped in. If nothing else, she reasoned, staring down into the hole might give her the closure she needed. Knox wouldn't let her go back, definitely not alone, for according to both him and Jason the spell might overpower her.

She considered how everything in her life had led to this moment—the very existence of the rift—even the tragedies of losing her baby, of Tiffany's life-taking. She saw Tiffany's note on the table where they'd left it before falling asleep, picked it up, and ran her fingers over the ink. What have you done? she wanted to ask Tiffany. What else could you want from me, after everything that's already been taken?

20

In his sleep, Knox dreamed of Tiffany. He had visited her lab, brought her lunch and flowers to congratulate her on a recent achievement. In the dream, her lab appeared more futuristic than he remembered—machines from a post-apocalyptic era, rusted piecemeal contraptions constructed from the shrapnel of a wreckage. He dreamt she was pregnant, her belly swollen, ready to pop. They smiled at each other, eating sushi with chopsticks, and Tiffany explained how she was to give birth with the assistance of one of the machines in the lab. Knox tried to convince her of the dangers of such an operation, but she assured him there was no other way. "This baby is coming out one way or another," she said, patting his hair and staring into his eyes, hers gray, like the girl's. She took him by the hand and guided him through the lab, which was powered hydraulically due to lack of electricity, as if it was Tiffany—not Margot—he'd been with after the quake.

At the birth machine, as Tiffany called it, Knox started to remember Margot. Had she been the one who killed herself? Fleeting as the thought of her face was, he was overcome with remorse, longing to return to real life. "I need to wake up now," he said, but Tiffany pressed a finger to his lips and told him to remain quiet, to wait for the birth machine to midwife a new reality for them both. She pressed a button, and the machine began to whir. Its robotic arms reached for Tiffany, lifted her onto an operating table. Smiling at Knox, she spread herself open and, without pain, allowed the machine to deliver their child.

He opened his eyes, the bright sunlight comforting, a reminder of the simple luxuries of life from before the blackout. Having nowhere to be on a weekend. Rolling over to feel the warmth of a lover. For a moment he indulged in a good stretch on the couch, the feeling of having overslept much needed after the past few days. All too quickly the memory of last night's conversation returned, Margot's speculations about Tiffany like something out of a science-fiction film.

And where was Margot? He got up, called her name, and checked every room, even inside the fort. Nowhere did he see her or Lane. He recalled her mentioning the first floor of the house. Maybe she's down there, he thought. He started for the door but stopped when he saw Tiffany's note on the kitchen table. Heart pounding, he wondered if Margot would have returned to the beach without him. Like a punch in the gut, the answer became evident. He flung the door open and rushed down the stairs, not even bothering to check the first floor. If she was at the beach, he didn't have any time to waste searching elsewhere.

His first thought: Where have all the people gone? Since they'd arrived at Jason's, Knox had barely seen anyone wandering the streets, going to or from their buildings. Not like back in Hollywood. Running toward the boardwalk, Venice looked more like a ghost town than the busy tourist destination he was used to. When the cleft came into view, he called out Margot's name again, though the winds from the shore muted his shouts. The beach was empty except for a few seagulls flying in the distance, the souvenir shops as deserted as when he'd first followed the girl here. With a double take, over the cries of the gulls and the howl of the wind, he heard barking—Lane. The dog's leash was tied to a signpost a few yards away from the crevice, but Margot was nowhere to be seen.

At the signpost, Knox knelt to Lane and let the dog lick his face. "Where'd she go, boy?" Lane stirred, eager to be free of the leash. If she left Lane here, there's only one place she could be, Knox thought. He turned around and looked at the rocks bulging out of the sand, the splice dividing what had once been flat, solid ground. He scratched behind Lane's ears and said, "Wait here for me, buddy." Wanting to leave behind a memento for Margot in case she hadn't followed Jason into the rift, or in case she happened to return before he did, he took off his wedding band, unfastened Lane's collar, and slid it onto the fabric. This will let her know I was here, he thought. This will let her know that I went in after her, that I had no other choice.

Sand and wind in his face, he started in the direction of the hole. Flooded with emotions and thoughts—How could Margot go through with it carrying their child? Would he ever see her face again? Had she gone in because she wanted to be with Jason?—he put one foot in front of the other, trudging through the sand until he was, at last, staring down the cavity. One look and he was again transfixed, the calm washing over him, the desire to free fall all-consuming.

Effortlessly, he put the final foot forward and began his descent.

PART 2

DESCENT

21

DARKNESS.

Violet light.

Jason stretched his limbs as far as he could in all directions, but he felt nothing except the wind from the free fall grazing his skin. Clear now that this abyss had no end, he opened his mouth and screamed.

No sound.

He tried to turn his body and face another direction, hoping light from the sky would still be visible, if only a speck.

No matter which way he turned, the darkness and the violet light remained fixed in his field of vision.

He questioned the possibility of his descent to the underworld.

Was this his price to pay for letting the girl take the plunge?

For the death of his unborn child?

The violet light grew closer, brighter. Jason felt the heat from the light cascade upon him. Faster than a blink the darkness diminished and Jason witnessed only light, an all-encompassing violet aura.

He was surrounded, and when he tried to look at his hands in front of him, he saw nothing but light. Was it that bright, that blinding, or had he disappeared?

He could not feel his flesh or the beating of his heart.

Just as quickly as the sound had been sucked into the void it came gushing back into his ears—the sound of the girl's voice, of her laughter. The violet light diminished and before him flashed images, like those on a movie screen, of him and the girl. And Margot. Memories that were not his own. A life he had not lived.

He saw himself pushing the girl on a swing, Margot on the other side, tapping the girl's feet. They smiled at each other as the girl pendulated back and forth, back and forth.

Younger, now—the girl running around the house with Margot chasing after her. Jason on his knees, arms wide open to catch the girl. The three of them topple upon the floor and fill the room with laughter. Laughter, bursting with such joy that Jason has never known. He looks into Margot's eyes, the girl's forehead at his lips, both of their hair tangled between his fingers. Tears form in his eyes, and he thanks God for this gift. This family.

Margot in a hospital bed, her belly swollen, doctors and nurses surrounding her. Beads of sweat dripping from her face as she clenches her teeth—and Jason, standing at her side, gripping her hand, wedding bands on both of their ring fingers. A baby emerging from Margot's body.

Their child.

The girl belonged to them.

Jason blinked and the moving images disappeared, replaced by the violet light. He felt as if he'd been woken from a deep sleep. His arms out in front of him, he tried to clutch at the life that was not there, the images that were but mere illusions. He remained suspended in the light, the laughter ringing in his ears, when a structure appeared before him. A frame. A doorway. Able to see his hands in front of him, the sensation of his body returning, he stepped forward.

The sky was violet. Unusual, Jason thought, but beautiful—more so than that boring blue one he remembered. He wasn't sure how long he'd been at the beach, sitting on a blanket with Margot and his daughter. Watching his daughter build sandcastles, he felt as if time had been at a standstill. Waves rolled upon the shore, other families and children standing waist-deep in the verdant ocean, their laughter as shrill as the cries of birds overhead. He looked around the beach for the opening that had been there only moments before. It was gone. Nothing but sand and beachgoers as far as he could see. The memory of the fall through the darkness began to feel like a dream, the reality of this new place lodging itself into his mind's eye—unquestionable, ever-existing.

Margot turned to face him, tilted her head, and peered over the rim of her sunglasses. She looked so good in her bathing suit—he wanted her right then and there. How long had it been since they'd last slept together?

"What do you say we go home and put her down for a nap?" Margot said, biting the end of her charcoal pencil flirtatiously. Jason saw on her sketchpad a near-perfect recreation of the boardwalk. "Once she's asleep we can cuddle for a while, if you catch my drift."

Jason couldn't remember Margot so happy, at least not since they'd moved to LA. In Florida, before life became too stressful, she'd embraced her sensuality, her amorousness. He'd known her to flash him on the beach if nobody was looking, but all that changed when she had gotten pregnant.

"Consider your drift caught," he said.

"What are you guys talking about?" His daughter's voice—it was like the first time he'd ever heard it, so small, frail, and yet so distinguished.

"Nothing, honey," Margot said, "Just grown-up things."

"Boring," the girl said. "I want someone to come and help me build a fortress. The biggest fortress in the world."

"Maybe your father will if you ask him nicely."

Being called a father gave Jason chills. "It's weird, that word. Father."

She tilted her head. "If it's still weird after having one kid, you'd better get used to it with another on the way."

Another?

Margot rolled onto her back, revealing her bulging belly.

He froze, both enamored and shocked.

"Are you okay?" Margot said. "Maybe you're getting too much sun. You want to pack up and head home?"

"I'm fine," he lied. "You're just so far along already. It's hard to believe."

"I don't want to go home," the girl said. She threw her pail toward the ocean and rolled face down in the sand.

"Your turn," Margot said. "I handled her last meltdown."

"Right," Jason said, eyes bouncing between Margot's yet-to-be-born child and the already-born one. He lay next to his daughter in the sand and kissed the back of her head.

"We're not going home yet, sweetheart. We can stay at the beach for a little while, okay?"

She looked up, face covered in sand and pieces of seashells. "I don't ever want to go home! I want to stay here forever. And I don't want to be a big sister. When Mommy has another baby, you're both going to forget about me."

"Oh, princess," he said. "We could never forget about you. Do you know when you were born it made Daddy happier than anything in the world?"

"But when the baby comes it's going to make you happier than I did."

In his daughter's moment of pain, he caught a resemblance, an expression of jealousy and insecurity, that neither belonged to him nor Margot.

The face of another person—another man—flashed through his mind and faded just as quickly.

"That's not true, buttercup. When your little brother or sister is born, it's going to make me equally as happy. No mommy or daddy can love their children differently. And you'll see—when you become a big sister, you're going to experience the same joy we felt when we got to become your parents."

His daughter's face scrunched, tears nearing.

"But will I be a good sister?"

"If you love and protect your brother or sister no matter what, even when they get annoying, then you'll be the best sister."

The girl looked up at the violet sky, squinted her eyes, and released the tension in her face. "I think I understand now. Hey! Who's going to help me wash all this sand off?" She stood up and wobbled toward the waves without concern as to whether one of her parents was behind her.

"Wait for your father!" Margot reached for Jason to help her up, the weight of her belly throwing her off balance. They chased after the girl until they were ankle-deep in the ocean. Margot warned the girl not to get saltwater in her eyes, and Jason, as if he'd been waiting to share this ancient wisdom, told Margot that their daughter will be okay no matter what, that some things are best learned the hard way.

22

As soon as Margot looked into the chasm, she knew Jason and Knox had been serious about its strange, magnetic power. One glance was all it took to bind her to the shadow, thick as wool, inviting as the water of the Florida Keys on a scorching summer day. Even though she'd already been determined to enter no matter the cost, she had to admit they were right. She did not have the strength to fight its call. Margot had known no greater serenity than succumbing to its pull. Had Tiffany felt the same the moment before kicking out the stepladder? Even though she carried the child inside her, Margot did not fear what harm would come from the fall. Perhaps this fearlessness was a testament to its power, to Tiffany's brilliance. Margot imagined herself an acrobat, plummeting after a microscopic misstep, knowing there would be a net beneath her to keep her from death.

How far down did the hole go? Hair strewn about, she lost the ability to gauge its depths, nothing in reach but total darkness and stale air and infinity. If Jason and the girl had jumped in, would she meet them at the bottom? Certainly, she hadn't already passed them, although she considered the fallibility of the laws of gravity given the nature of Tiffany's experiment. Perhaps they were all down in the abyss simultaneously, falling over and over again, non-stop throughout all of time. Knox would discover that she'd jumped soon enough, and he would come after her. The three of them—four counting the child in her belly, five counting the little girl—would be suspended in the void for the rest of eternity if they should be so lucky. This must be what it feels like in the birth canal, Margot thought, stretching her fingers and toes as if to embrace the walls of a womb. "A perfect circle," she said, though no sound was made. "The cycle of life and death." She looked at her hands and saw they had begun to glow a bright shade of purple. Waving them around, bright purple lines trailed in the darkness like motion blur, art created by the purest of paints, that holy material which God created before all else.

Light.

Her hands did not burn, and the brighter they shone the less black the hole became. Soon it was all scorched with violet. Her body was no more; nor, by proxy, was the body of her child. This cannot be heaven, she thought, for I hear no choir of angels. Nor can this be hell, for I feel no fire. At once Margot accepted that she was the root of all illumination, every light that had ever carved out the world's shadows. A woman, a mother. Releasing the child from her belly as unlimited radiance, she felt herself merging with the innards of the earth itself.

A new voice came to her, spoke to her from within, as a spirit would. The voice asked her what she wanted now that she had reached the point of no return. Margot answered in thought: I wish the best for my children, for their fathers, and my soul. The voice promised to grant her wish in exchange for her light, a trade she was hesitant to make. She asked: If I gift you my light, am I forever doomed to darkness?

Forever is what you make it, the voice replied, and darkness may only exist in the absence of light.

Margot nodded and instantly felt her heart opening, a safe that had been locked since what seemed the dawn of time. All that was left of her essence, her energy, eviscerated. Evaporated. Destroyed and recycled into the endlessness of the cosmos.

23

THE BREATH KNOCKED out of him, cold air blanketing his skin, Knox soon saw nothing but darkness and the faint glow of violet light. A vacuum, he thought. This isn't a hole in the ground, but a vortex. Jason, the girl, Margot, Tiffany—their faces flashed through Knox's mind until the violet light surrounded him, and all their faces—all the faces he'd ever seen, his face—became one face. The one face with eyes glowing violet, pupils the rift itself. Suspended, the feeling of levitation now like second nature, he could not tell how long he'd been away from the world above. His body—did he have one, anymore?—was more an ethereal presence, one with everything as perceived by the set of violet eyes, the One Face. Its mouth opened, more black than the rift itself, and Knox understood it was a doorway, a gate, the very entry point toward which his entire life led.

Tiffany's voice, as if in an echo chamber, ricocheted through his head. Broken sound bites from things she had said to him in life, in the dream with the birth machine, and from her suicide note overlapped until the One Face transformed into hers. The only way to silence her, Knox realized, was to step into her mouth, permit the void of her to swallow him.

Knox couldn't believe what he saw: Tiffany, walking toward him in the sand, holding the hand of a little girl. They both smiled and waved. The girl looked up to Tiffany, asked something. Tiffany nodded. The girl let go of Tiffany's hand and ran for Knox, the waves lapping at her bare feet. He held his arms open out of pure instinct, a gesture he'd done hundreds of times before. Upon impact, the girl felt like a missing puzzle piece in Knox's arms—she felt like home. Her arms wrapped tight around him, he looked down into her eyes, bright violet, two round amethysts. The girl said, "I love you, Daddy." His face grew hot, tears forming instantly. Once Tiffany was in reach, he pulled her close, the girl sandwiched between them. Huddled together, the breeze intensified upon his wet face, Knox wondered what he had done to merit this moment of bliss.

Tiffany reeled back, her hair dancing in the wind, and placed her hand on Knox's neck. "We were wondering where you were," she said. Knox wasn't sure what she meant, the thought of another woman lingering like a reverie, her name on the tip of his tongue.

Marie.

Margaret?

The girl took Knox and Tiffany in each hand and led them toward the water. "We're going to play a game," she said. "I'll be the Little Mermaid. Daddy can be King Triton, and Mommy can be Ursula."

"Ursula?" Tiffany laughed, reached down to tickle the girl, making her squeal and swat at the incoming waves. "Come on, King Triton, you've got a mermaid to save!" She picked up the girl and carried her out further. Knox waded in slowly, the image of the two playing together forging itself into his subconscious, the purity of which he felt undeserving.

The girl leaped from Tiffany's arms and splashed toward Knox. "You can't get me, Sea Witch! I'm going home!"

Go home, he thought. Those words...

Knox couldn't help but to dive forward, give in to their game of pretend. Before he knew it, the sun had begun to set, the sky turned vibrant shades of emerald, fuchsia—a bizarre amalgam of colors colliding in the fashion of the Northern Lights. They returned to the shore and walked across the beach without their shoes. Knox looked down at their three sets of feet, caked in sand, and realized he had never been so connected to the earth. It was then that he remembered the schism, the very rupture in the ground that brought him here.

Was it real, or merely conjured from his imagination?

"Are you feeling alright?" It was Tiffany, whispering as to not alarm the girl.

"Some nausea," he lied. "Must have swallowed a bit of saltwater."

"Saltwater taffy," the girl said, giggling and trying to make way for the candy shop on the boardwalk.

"Not before dinner, you little mermaid," Tiffany said.

The girl continued hopping and kicking up sand. "After dinner?"

"You'll have to ask your father."

The girl looked up at him with those amethyst eyes. As if he could say no.

"If you eat all your veggies."

She stuck out her tongue, and he stuck his out right back. She sniggered and broke away from him and Tiffany, yelling,

"You can't catch me!" Knox ran after her and made monster noises, chasing her in circles around Tiffany.

"Alright, you two," Tiffany said. "Mommy's getting dizzy."

Knox picked the girl up and put her on his shoulders. "You're getting big, girl. I won't be able to do this much longer."

"Nope! I'm going to stay little forever and ever."

"Forever is what you make it," Tiffany said.

Knox had to double take. Where had he heard that phrase before?

"Did you make that up?"

"Kind of just came to me," she said.

"Darkness may only exist in the absence of light," he said, more out of force than choice.

"I'm scared of the dark," the girl said. "Last night I dreamed I fell into a big dark hole in the beach. I went down and down and when I came out I was by this statue and a man found me."

"Was it the bogeyman?" Tiffany sounded nonchalant as if the girl's dream had been recurring.

"No, this time it was a nice man. He took me to his house and kept me safe from all the scary people, and then Daddy showed up, but he was with another lady."

Tiffany cocked her eyebrow and smacked him on the arm. "Another lady, huh?"

"I swear I have no idea what she's talking about." He remembered, though, as if he'd somehow shared the dream with his daughter. That name on the tip of his tongue: Marilyn? Marjory?

"Nobody ever knows what I'm talking about," the girl said.

Knox and Tiffany laughed.

"Spoken like the daughter of a physicist," Tiffany said.

They strolled along the boardwalk and Knox bought his daughter a handful of taffy which, he guaranteed, would only be eaten after a nutritious dinner. As the sky darkened and the boardwalk lit up with lights from the surrounding shops, Knox forgot about the schism he'd imagined on the beach, and the name he couldn't remember faded from his mind.

K.,

The memories returned quicker than expected.

The first thing I realized was cold water around my legs, sand beneath my feet. I was holding something small, delicate. A little girl's hand. The sun was so bright I could hardly see. When I saw the man who always plays guitar while he roller-skates, I realized it was Venice Beach. I walked forward, carefully leading the girl until she let go of me and started running. At first, I panicked. And then I realized she was running to you.

You pulled me close to you; the little girl was in between us. Everything felt uncanny, as if it were real but also a dream.[∞] *I reached out to touch your*

[∞] The narrative of dreams is such that the beginning of the dream is not necessarily a logical narrative starting point. For when we begin to find ourselves within a dream-in-motion, logic is not needed to continue further into the narrative. We do not need to question how we began because the scenario in which we have found ourselves existing is a plausible-enough construct to our minds that improvisation becomes natural, even without knowledge of the past. This is what coming into my body, into my mind, was like in that moment. The reality of you and me with child was plausible enough for me to proceed without question.

neck and, for a moment, you looked confused. Suddenly a familiar comfort came over me. The sensation of consistency. The little girl—our daughter—wanted to play. We appeased her until it was time to go home for dinner. Something had come over you, a bug of some type. I nursed you as best I could, and it all started to come back to me.

The rift.

The passage through the black hole.

Once I realized what was happening, that I had awoken to an entirely different version of my reality, I knew I had to tell you.

Despite everything you did, I couldn't betray you.

But perhaps I told you too soon.

You told me you had dreamt I was dead.

It made me question what I had done.

How many realities were there?

You told me I had taken my own life.

More memories started to rush into my mind all at once.

I saw what I had done to myself.

I could see it clearly in my mind.

Yet, somehow, I couldn't understand how it had come to pass.

Not when the last thing I remembered before the beach was going through the rift.

But then it dawned on me.

The fact was, in our memory, the multiple realities had converged only in the mind's eye.

It could be said both of these statements are simultaneously true:

You inherently had experienced losing me to suicide, although it was not in the Coil that we were currently occupying.

I had inherently not experienced death by suicide but could remember the experience from a separate Coil.

To think: There is a variable of my existence that contains suicide. But the constants never change, K. It was inevitable for me to create the black hole. It was inevitable for me to choose to go through it.[∞] *In doing so, I left one reality behind for another. It seems no matter which reality we are in, that will always be a constant.*

I soon realized all of this knowledge would vanish. For you and me. The longer we existed after the event horizon, the more whatever happened before it would cease to exist in our minds.

[∞] But is it possible for me to truly know if I went through the black hole? I have memories of the year leading up to the production of the event horizon, but I also have memories that line up with the one you claimed to remember, the one in which I died by my own hand. I'm afraid I can no longer decipher what really happened; it is most accurate to say that both versions of these stories happened and more.

It seemed unfair for me to have forced this life upon you.

And I now know, if there is a God, why He has given us all free will.

Because the love we receive is nothing if its giver has not chosen to do so.

But then I thought of a way to possibly break the cycle.

And for some reason, the forgiving side of me decided to share this with you.

So that the choice could be yours.

24

JASON, MARGOT, AND the girl stayed up watching movies and playing Chutes & Ladders. No matter how many rules she had to break, the girl would not let Jason win. "You can't go down the chute, only up," she'd said, knocking his piece off the board.

"One of these days you're going to have to learn to play by the rules," he said.

"Nope, not me," the girl said, sliding her piece all over the table. She leaped up from her seat and went into the living room where she sat on the floor next to her box of toys.

"She ought to be asleep in twenty or less," Margot said. She put her hand on his knee and rubbed his thigh.

"I know it sounds weird," he said, "but I feel like I haven't seen you in a long time. Like I woke up today out of a coma." He wanted to ask her about the expression he'd caught on their daughter's face earlier at the beach. The one he'd have sworn he once saw on another man. Instead, he put his hand on hers, squeezed her fingers, brought them to his face, and kissed them.

"You've seen me every day for years," she said, deadpan. "I'm surprised you're not tired of me by now."

"Don't say that. I could never tire of you, or her. Our family." He pressed his other hand to her stomach. A tiny vibration pulsed under his fingers—the baby kicking.

Margot smiled. "Someone can't wait to meet you," she said.

Jason noticed the silence in the living room—their daughter had fallen asleep while playing with her toys. "Shall I take her to her room?"

"Oh yeah. She's out for the night." Margot stood from the table, curled her finger under his chin, and let it trail across his lips as she walked away. He couldn't help but stare at her butt and legs; she looked sexier than ever. Was it the fact that she was carrying yet another one of his children? Urges tore through him, enough to rush tucking their daughter in so he could follow Margot to the bedroom where she already lay across the bed, skin aglow in candlelight, wearing only lingerie.

"That was fast," he said.

"Every second counts." She rubbed her hand in circles over the comforter. "Now get over here before I drag you."

He could no longer resist her. His blood pumped. He went erect. She reached for him and undid his pants. In the flickering light, her bulbous stomach glimmered, copper-colored like the moon during a lunar eclipse. He ran his hands over her smooth skin, wrapped her hair around his fingers. Wanting to synthesize with her every molecule and entangle himself in her forever, he couldn't escape the feeling that it was all a dream.

"Are you here? If I close my eyes, will you disappear?"

"Enough silliness," she said and leaned in to kiss him.

He closed his eyes and reopened them. She was still there, her heat radiating upon him, her eyes staring back. He thought he saw her irises flash violet—a trick of the candlelight?—and was drawn into the darkness of her pupils. His gaze now locked, he felt the rush of vertigo and a familiar sensation of free falling without end, suspended and breathless.

25

MARGOT AWOKE TO the bite of cold water at her feet, having just avoided a dream in which she was drowning. Heart racing, she lifted her head and realized she was at the beach, lying in the sand. In front of her, two children—girls—sat in the water, the bigger one splashing the smaller one.

"Be nice to your sister," Margot said. She noted the tingle of annoyance rising through her, tired of having to remind her eldest daughter of common courtesies.

"But Mom, Tiffany never wants to play," the older one said. "She's been sitting here staring at the waves the whole time."

Tiffany—hearing the name gave Margot the fleeting sensation of déjà vu.

"Where is your father?" she said.

"You can't erase the past," the older girl said under her breath.

Margot did a double take. Why did that phrase strike a chord in her?

From whom had she before heard it? It produced a pang in her gut, that of remorse and envious wrath.

"Excuse me?"

Her daughter tilted her head. "I thought you told us not to talk about him?"

Had she? Margot couldn't remember making such a request. She scanned the beach for him but realized she couldn't quite picture his face.

Margot recognized the emptiness of loss behind the girl's eyes. But she also recognized the gaze of someone else, a person she'd long forgotten.

"Bring your sister over here," she said.

"Tiffany, come on," the girl shouted. "Mom wants to talk to you."

The little one rose from where she sat and slowly slumped over, hanging her head in full pout.

"What's the matter, love?" Margot reached under Tiffany's chin so that their gaze met. Tiffany's amber eyes streamed with tears; her tiny chest heaved to suppress the sound of her sobs.

"I don't want Roxie to hear me because she'll make fun of me," Tiffany whispered.

"Roxana, give us a few minutes alone. Go down by the water and stay where I can see you."

"Fine," Roxana said, swinging her arms with attitude.

"Now tell me, my love." Margot patted Tiffany's wet hair, trying to get the girl to smile.

"I just wanted to go back to the way things were." She averted any eye contact.

"What do you mean? What don't you like about the way things are now?"

"We weren't always here. Before everything got different. I don't want to pretend. I don't want to lie to you."

Margot sat up straight and tried to think about what their lives were like before this moment, but she couldn't remember. Her memory was hazy, a fog she could not lift.

"You don't have to lie to me," Margot said. "You should always tell me the truth, just as I will always tell you the truth."

Tiffany looked at the sky, took a deep breath, and calmed her sobs. "Okay," she said. "You're not going to like it. You're going to be mad at me. But I'm the reason we're here. I built it. You know the earthquake?"

Margot dug her fingers into the sand. She vaguely remembered an earthquake, but the thought felt more like someone else's, a story she'd heard rather than an experience she'd lived through.

"I don't know when the last earthquake was," she said.

"Yes, you do," Tiffany said. She sat down next to Margot. "I know you remember. It changed everything. There was a big rumble, and then the power went out. You didn't know where to go so you came to the beach and then went down the hole."

The hole—Margot closed her eyes, the darkness from her eyelids helping her channel a distant memory. The sensation of falling overcame her, and upon opening her eyes she was hit with vertigo.

"I think I remember something," Margot said. "A sinkhole."

"Nope," Tiffany said. "It wasn't that. It was more like a fissure. Trust me, I made it."

How did she know the difference between a fissure and a sinkhole? Margot looked at the child, but she still avoided direct eye contact.

"What do you mean you made it?"

"I mean in the other life," Tiffany said. "Before I died."

Margot withdrew her fingers from the sand and took hold of Tiffany's face, squeezing her cheeks and turning her head so that she had no choice but to look at her.

“Where is all this coming from?” she demanded. “Where are you getting this? Did you hear your sister talking about death? Was it on television?”

“Please don’t get mad,” Tiffany said. “If you think real hard, you’ll remember. Before we came here, I died. I promise I’m not lying. This place, where we are now, wasn’t always here. It was a different life before. I made the earthquake happen, and the hole in the ground, and I figured out how to make it so I wouldn’t be dead anymore.”

Margot stood up and yanked Tiffany off her butt. “Roxana, get over here,” she called to her other daughter. “You need to tell me right now what you said to your sister.”

“No, please,” Tiffany pleaded. “Roxie doesn’t know anything about this. I promise.”

Margot couldn’t respond to the child. She waited until she had both girls by the hand and looked around the beach again. Where had their father gone?

“You’re not going to find him,” Tiffany said. “He’s not here.”

“What is she talking about, Roxana?” Roxana’s eyes were wild, her mouth agape. Margot realized that she was gripping both of them too tight.

“Dad’s dead,” Roxana said. “He killed himself.”

Margot released them, stepped backward, and nearly toppled over.

Visions of a man came to the forefront of her mind—a man smiling, a man holding her daughters, a man’s warm hands caressing her face. Before she knew it, she’d fallen into the sand, and more memories flashed by: a man telling her this is not goodbye, a man’s limp body spread across their daughters’ bedroom floor, a man’s expressionless eyes peering up at her. In each memory she gathered only a vague recollection of a man, his face blurry, out of focus. She felt her daughters' hands against her skin, their heat retrieving her from the cold depths of remembrance.

"Are you okay, Mommy?" Margot opened her eyes to find Roxana staring at her, cradling her face. Beside Roxana, Tiffany sat in the sand with Margot's hand clenched in hers.

"I'm fine now," Margot said. "Must be the heat. It's time for us to go home." She staggered to her feet with the help of her daughters and asked them to gather their belongings. While they made haste picking up towels and beach toys, Margot struggled to keep her balance. The rays from the setting sun cast a golden glow upon her children and, as she squinted to watch them, she finally remembered the face of their father.

Dear Margot,

So much can be said of the power of the periphery.

To see a person from a completely different vantage point can change your entire understanding of them.

At first, I thought I was dreaming.

A sister? A mother? The ocean? And I was so little.

It started to come back to me when I heard you and Roxana talking about our father. I recognized you, yet I did not. You called me over to you, and I did as you asked. I was afraid to upset you. As soon as you put your hand on my face, I knew. That you were not my mother. At least not in the sense that we naturally think of mothers.

Upon looking into your eyes, a surge of envy and spite and rage flowed through me. A thirst for revenge so hot I thought you'd feel it on your fingertips. But then you began to speak to me, and the sound of your voice was a salve to the burning. Your voice carried such warmth, such love. It created in me a deeper longing for you, a stronger sense of trust.

That sense of trust is what guided me to reveal everything to you. Even now, all this time later, I'm not sure if I made the right decision. I told you about the earthquake and the rift. I told you about the suicide. In this reality, it was not mine. But by now you may realize that it is a constant for us—one way or another. In this reality, it was someone you loved. And it was not something that could be undone. Telling you about this death almost made you faint. Even then, in that little body, I couldn't handle knowing the amount of grief I'd caused you.

It was strange, explaining to you what I knew while your mind was still unable to process the transformation you'd made. Even now, I'm still unsure of how the memories returned the way they did. I thought by now I would have forgotten all I knew before going through the rift, but the memories still cling to me like moths to light. The more I started to tell you about him, the more your memories from before the rift returned.

As did the love you felt.

And this is why I tried to undo the Coil.

I tried, Margot.

I tried to straighten the line of time.

But I'm not so sure I succeeded.

26

After dinner, Knox, Tiffany, and their daughter played with a kids' science lab kit and ate taffy. Knox watched Tiffany and the girl mix glue, food coloring, and Borax into a plastic container with their hands until it molded into slime. Sitting at the dining room table, Knox couldn't believe the turns his life had taken. He looked around the room at the pictures on the walls—him and Tiffany before the baby was born, the baby at every stage of life leading to the present.

"What are you waiting for, Daddy?" The girl raised her hands to show him what he was missing out on.

"Just marveling at my loves," he said. "My two scientists." He winked at Tiffany and stuck his hands into the freshly formed slime. Its bright violet slightly mirrored his daughter's amethyst eyes, and when she glanced up at him with a silly grin, it was all he could do to not devolve into a substance much like the goo at his fingertips.

After the slime had been put away and all the taffy was eaten, the girl insisted upon a round of hide-and-seek.

"You're all hopped up on sugar, aren't you, Margot?" Tiffany knelt and kissed the girl's forehead. "We have your father to blame for that."

Margot. That was the name that had been on the tip of his tongue at the beach. Suddenly he remembered saying the name aloud to the nurse after Tiffany gave birth. Tiffany had been the one to suggest it, and Knox couldn't deny how perfectly it fit.

"I'd love a good game of hide-and-seek," Knox said, peering fiendishly at Tiffany through squinted eyes. "Can we play in the dark?"

Margot's face beamed. "Nope," she said, running into the other room in desperate search of a hiding place. "I'm afraid of the dark!"

Tiffany looked at him and pursed her lips. "Well, my authority has been undermined. This can only mean one thing."

Knox stammered an attempt to form an apology.

Tiffany stepped forward. "You're it!" She stuck out her tongue and followed Margot into the other room. "Daddy's it! He has to count to sixty!"

Knox raced from one to ten, jumped to sixty, and yelled, "Ready or not, here I come!" He heard a shriek from a different room and high-pitched giggling coming from under the table.

"I wonder where my little girl could be?" He purposefully put his toes beneath the table. "She's probably...in the refrigerator!"

Margot squealed and said, "Silly Daddy! There's no way I could fit in there."

"You just gave yourself away, pumpkin." He got on all fours to meet Margot on the carpet. "Let's find Mommy and then it's time for bed."

She climbed out and took him by the hand. "I know where she is. Be very, very quiet."

He nodded and followed her to the bedroom. Margot pointed to the closet and whispered, "She's in there."

The closet. Knox felt sick in his stomach. His throat tightened. An image of a woman hanging from a rope passed through his mind. A long-forgotten nightmare, or a dormant part of his imagination?

"Go ahead," Margot said. "She's waiting for you."

Knox shook his head, took a step back. "I can't."

The girl cocked her head. "But you're it."

Words formulated in his head: *Your final chance to hold me*. He nearly said the words aloud but bit the side of his cheek to cease them. Where had he heard them before?

He told the girl to find her mother, that he wasn't feeling well and needed to sit down. She frowned and nodded, releasing his hand as he went into the living room. Now the walls and the pictures mounted on them spun around him.

"Margot told me something was wrong with you." He felt Tiffany's hand on his shoulder but couldn't look up for fear of vomiting. "I'm going to put her to bed and come right back. Here, drink this." She set a glass of water on the table, but he feared he wouldn't be able to keep it down. He simply nodded and closed his eyes.

But in the darkness behind his lids, he saw the woman again—strands of her blonde hair between his fingers, rope constricted beneath her bluing face.

The coil of unbecoming death.

He stood, rushed to the toilet, spat up dinner and taffy. Face hot with tears, he sank to the linoleum, lay sideways until he looked up and saw Tiffany rapidly searching through the medicine cabinet.

"I'm fine," he said. "Really. Just got too much sun." He tried to pull himself up using the sink.

"You don't look fine. I need you to take this. Open your mouth." He did. She put in two pills. "Should help with dizziness and nausea. Drink." She held up the glass of water from the table, now with a straw sticking out, which seemed to find its way into his mouth. He gulped enough to swallow the pills and sank back down to the floor. Tiffany put the back of her hand to his forehead, said that he was burning up, and helped him stand to walk to the couch. She told him to lie down, wait for her to get him a cold rag. He nodded, feared closing his eyes again for what he might see.

Suddenly their house felt unfamiliar to him, the lavender-colored walls like something from a film he'd seen long ago. When did they move into this house? When did they leave The Libra? Had it been before or after Margot was born? He couldn't remember. The blur of transitions impossible to make clear, he couldn't fight the need to let his eyes rest. Heavy curtains closing over his mind, the darkness brought him back to the closet. The lifeless woman. The weight of her in his arms as he cut her down from the anchor point she'd fixed in the ceiling. His throat hoarse from screaming her name, screaming for help. Her limp body like a doll when he lay her on the floor. His desperate prayers to God to bring her back to him. The rush of anxiety to take his own life as he waited for the ambulance to come and claim her.

A cold twinge against his head. His eyes jolted open and he gasped for breath.

"It's okay." Tiffany pressed the rag evenly across his forehead. "Just keep this here for a little while, then I'll take your temperature."

"Where's Margot?" Two images raced through his mind: Margot as a child and Margot as a grown woman.

"She's asleep," Tiffany said. "I told you I put her to bed ten minutes ago."

"Right. It feels like longer." He could no longer resist the weight of his eyelids. Tiffany told him to get some rest, that she wouldn't leave his side. But as he emerged again into the nightmare, he knew she was wrong, that she had long left his side. In the nightmare he watched the paramedics roll her away, her body beneath a white sheet. He shook with grief and rage when they brought him in for questioning. He remained calm when her father tried to choke him. He drank whiskey until he was numb and helped her parents with the arrangements to get her body from California to Ohio. He knew that it was his fault, though in the nightmare he couldn't quite recall what he'd done to push Tiffany to hang herself.

Margot.

A miscarriage.

In the nightmare, he couldn't picture his daughter, but he saw a woman and a man weeping, the woman holding her belly. Knox wanted to wake up, but the darkness had ensnared him, the fever dream digging deeper into his mind. He now felt something coil around his neck—Tiffany's father's hands? The noose?—and the quick sinking feeling after leaping from a high dive. Only there came no splash, no immersion. Only falling. An incessant plunge into nothingness.

"Wake up."

Tiffany, her hands shaking him out of the darkness.

"There's something I have to tell you."

"Our daughter," Knox muttered. "Is she okay?"

"She's okay, Knox, but you should know that none of this is real. Not real unless you want it to be."

Was he still dreaming? He pushed her hands aside and slowly rose from his sideways position on the couch.

"I have to see our daughter. I have to go to her."

"It's not necessary," Tiffany said. "Do you understand what I'm trying to tell you? This isn't real. Think hard. Try to remember where you were before the beach today."

"I dreamt that you were dead, Tiffany." He tried to stand but he nearly fell over the coffee table. "You took your own life. It was horrible, the worst thing I'd ever felt."

She grabbed his hand and pulled him back down to the couch. "Are you sure it was a dream? Or was it a memory? Tell me where you were before the beach."

He withdrew his hand from hers. He had the suspicion that she was playing some kind of cruel joke on him. What did she mean none of this was real? Maybe they had both gotten too much sun.

"I was with you and our daughter," he said. "And I don't know if you're trying to mess with my head or if we both have a fever, but either way I think we ought to call it a night."

"This isn't a joke, Knox. And it wasn't a dream. Listen to your heart and try to remember. Before this, in the other life, I died. My heart was broken, and I committed suicide. But before I did, I made it so we would all have another chance. I created the rift. The blackout led you and Margot to the beach. That was where I coordinated the event horizon. The rift, the hole in the ground, was a gateway that brought you here."

The violet slime in the container on the table caught Knox's eye. That color, when he looked at it all the sounds around him seemed to vanquish. Everything else in his field of vision faded away. He felt the color pulsating as if it were a part of his biology. Tiffany's words, like the color violet, reverberated through him. The memories from the dream replayed through his mind, all of them tinted with violet. He could not picture where he'd been before the beach. It was as if, somehow, time had started there, where the sand met the water. But if that were true, where had all the memories of Tiffany and their daughter come from?

If there had ever been a line between dreams and reality, it was no longer apparent to Knox. He realized he had started to shake, that Tiffany was staring at him, her face calm as the surface of a pond. Meanwhile, he felt a downpour of emotions—rage, remorse, regret—and if he couldn't soon get a grip, he would drown in them.

"You're fucking with me," he said. "I need a Klonopin or something."

"You have to make a choice, Knox. It won't be easy." Tiffany reached for a pencil and pad of paper on the table. She carefully drew what looked like a half-circle, and then another one slightly above it. At the end of the two lines, she drew a little head, and Knox understood that it was meant to be a snake. "The ouroboros," she said. The snake was ingesting its tail.

"Do you remember when I first explained it to you? In the other life? It was the basis for my research about black holes."

He remembered when she had tried to help him understand. It was years ago, before their daughter was born. They had just finished making love, and Tiffany was excited about recent funding in the physics department.

"Yes," he said. "I remember. But it wasn't another life, Tiffany. It's always been the same life."

She shook her head. "When mine ended, yours continued, until you and Margot went through the rift. Now there are multiple lives. This is what I've been trying to tell you, Knox. The history you remember is now spliced between what happened in the other life and what I manifested for us in this one. But they won't coexist for long. Soon your memories from the other life will fade. Unless you choose to go back. I can't force you to stay here. I wondered if you would even enter the rift at all, or if you and your wife would die before you found it. But you kept your promise from that day at the lake."

He remembered the cold air against his skin as he tasted her for the first time.

"Even hell couldn't keep me away," he said.

"I wanted to lead you both here," Tiffany said, "which is why I sent the child out when the rift opened. But you wouldn't believe what she had to do—the sacrifice she had to make—to exist on your side. You see, that which hasn't existed has a chance to do so here. All I needed was a small bit of DNA, which was easy to obtain after you had her in our home. The girl you met out there, the one with the gray eyes who first went into the rift, would have been your wife's if she hadn't miscarried. That's why the girl was drawn to Margot. In Margot's new life, which runs parallel to this one, she has two daughters. One for what she lost before you, and one for what she lost when she entered the rift. We have our daughter, our Margot, in this life because your wife was pregnant before you got here."

Knox now thought of the pregnancy test Margot had tried to hide from him before the earthquake.

"But she likely won't be the only fruit we bear," Tiffany continued. "Before I went, there was something I didn't tell you."

Knox's throat tightened.

"Tiffany, I—"

She gently raised her hand to stop him from speaking.

"I'm sorry, Knox. It took me this long to realize how selfish I am. At my core. Some things, it seems, we never change. Until it's too late."

Knox evaded her gaze, looked up into the ceiling light, and let the tears fall.

"It doesn't make sense," he said. "How was she my wife there and is my child here?" He couldn't believe what he was asking, that there was a possibility Tiffany's wild joke was real.

But he couldn't deny that his mind felt interwoven with memories. He couldn't reject that everything Tiffany had just said rang true, resonated somewhere deep within him, as though the experiences had happened moments ago.

"Because there are infinite planes of existence," Tiffany said. "There are realities upon realities upon realities. In a given reality, the variables may change but the constants never do. Every person's reality is subjective to their existence. Margot is one of the constants in your existence. I am, too. But your relationship to each constant varies within each reality. When we enter a black hole, there is no telling how the variables will change. In the reality where your other Margot currently resides, I am her daughter. Though, in the reality where you currently reside, I am her mother. In the reality you just came from, I am the ex-lover of her husband."

Knox peered over the couch and tried to glimpse into Margot's bedroom. A violet glow from her nightlight shone through the crack in the doorway. He had seen her born into this world through the eyes of a father, but he had also seen her through the eyes of a lover. Gut qualmish, he thought, Please, God—wake me from this dream.

"What did you mean my memories will fade unless I choose to go back?" He felt attached to all of the memories—those of him and Tiffany watching their daughter grow, and those of knowing that he and Margot had a child on the way. But each set of memories, each life, came coupled with both love and pain. He could not choose one without losing another.

"There is only a small amount of time left before you forget everything from the other life. But you may choose to go back before you lose them."

"What would I have to do to go back? Do I go back through the rift?"

She closed her eyes. "There is only one way back. You must do what I did. You must make the ultimate sacrifice."

The ultimate sacrifice.

Knox pictured her hanging from the rope.

"Is there another way?"

"I'm afraid not," she said. "The method you choose doesn't matter, so long as you die in this reality by your hand."

He wanted to ask her if hanging herself was merely a way to escape their old reality and enter a new one. Had she been so certain the act would guarantee a seamless transition? Surely no one could make such a choice without questioning whether they were about to leap into a bottomless void, even with an encyclopedic knowledge of theoretical physics at their disposal.

"I don't know what to believe," he said. "How long do I have?"

"You have until the last memory fades. There's no telling how long it will take."

"I remember that I wronged you," he said. "We had everything—apparently more than everything—and I still had an affair." His face grew hot, lips trembling. "You didn't deserve that, Tiffany. If I needed more, or something new, I didn't have to go behind your back. You gave me the world. You did nothing but love me. And I betrayed you. You and our…our—" he stuttered, couldn't bring himself to say the word 'child.' "Telling you I'm sorry doesn't take it back. I know that. But I never thought that it would affect you so deeply, that you would—"

"Say no more," she said. "I didn't exactly go quietly. None of that matters now. You can't erase the past."

You can't erase the past.

He'd said that to Margot, in the other life, when he caught her deleting photos of Tiffany from his computer. And how hypocritical he'd been, so overcome with jealousy when he learned that Margot and Jason nearly had a baby.

Jason.

Knox recalled the name but couldn't picture a face. Jason had entered the rift before Knox, and Margot must have entered after Jason. Knox wondered if the two of them were together in her reality.

"Margot has two daughters in her reality," Knox said, still trying to piece together Tiffany's explanation of them all. The infinite planes of existence. "Something tells me I'm not the father."

Tiffany took Knox's hand and placed the paper with the ouroboros drawing in it. The snake's single eye seemed to be staring into him with ambivalence.

"For any role that you could play in her life," Tiffany said, "there is a reality for it, unfolding at this very moment. We all have different parts to play in each go-around—parent, child, lover, friend, enemy, betrayer. I can tell you that where your Margot is—the same Margot who stole you from me—she will know the same torrent of memories. In some way, I will be there to explain it to her. I will tell her the same thing I told you: if you wish to return to the way things were, you must make a choice. If you hesitate to act, the memories will fade. It is true that where she is, she has both her children. Why would she want to leave when she has all of what she lost? Whether you are their father or not, it may soon make no difference to her once she has forgotten what came before the rift. Besides, you are one of her constants. She has you there with her, in some form or other."

He thought about Margot's incarnation in this reality. Perhaps his incarnation in her reality had taken a similar shape.

"And what if I make the choice but she doesn't?" Knox said. "Will I ever see her again?"

"Just as I had no way of knowing if I would see you again on this side of the rift, there is no telling what choice she will make in her reality."

Knox crumpled the paper in his hand and cast it into the container of violet slime. He turned away from Tiffany, unable to look at her.

"I don't understand how this is possible," he said. "I feel like I'm trapped in a nightmare. If I go back, but she doesn't, then I'll have lost you both."

"Which is why you have the choice to stay here. With me. Our child. Possibly another. Our family. Here, you can have it all."

Knox stood and went to their daughter's bedroom door. He nudged it open and saw her sleeping in the dim glow of her violet nightlight.

Yes, here he could have it all.

But would it be the same?

Would it be real?

27

Jason awoke to violet beams of light coming through the bedroom window. He still smelled Margot on his skin, but when he rolled over, nobody was there.

"Margot?" His throat was dry, eyes heavy. He knew they had stayed up late making love, but he couldn't remember what time they'd fallen asleep. Jason hadn't wanted to close his eyes for fear of waking up to find her gone.

He called her name again, rose from the bed with a sheet draped around him. The door opened slowly. Just as he expected to see Margot, a little girl popped her head through and sprang toward him.

"Daddy!"

She jumped into his arms and he fell backward into the bed.

Roxana, he thought. Roxie. My daughter.

He remembered putting her to bed the night before, how she'd kissed him goodnight. Somehow, she looked inches taller.

Then, upon closer examination of her face, he noticed how much she'd matured, grown, since the previous day. And in her maturation, he saw more clearly—or was it a trick of the mind, of having woken abruptly?—the visage of the other man who flickered into and out of his thoughts when he'd tried to console Roxie at the beach.

Though this recognition caused dormant envy to flare up in him, he couldn't resist the innocent, loving gaze of his child.

"My angel," he said, smiling as her frizzy hair tickled his chin.

The door opened again and, expecting to see Margot, a second little girl came running in, smaller than Roxie.

"Hey," she cried, "I want in here, too!"

"Tiffany's always interrupting my daddy time," Roxie pouted.

"Be nice to your sister," Margot called from down the hall.

The littlest one leaped onto the bed, knocking the wind out of Jason.

"You were supposed to come and wake me up, Daddy," she said. "But now I'm coming to wake you up. No more bad dreams, Daddy." She kissed him gently on the cheek.

He held the girls close to his chest. From where had the second one come? Had he slept away entire years of his life? The girls begged him to play with them, led him into the living room, each grabbing one of his hands.

The living room was lit up by a Christmas tree, all the presents beneath it already unwrapped. The girls talked over each other, exclaiming which toys were their favorites and which they were willing to trade. When Margot entered the room with a heaping plate of toast, Jason got up and took her into the kitchen.

"I need to know what's going on," he said, lifting her shirt to find that her belly was flat. "Where did she come from?"

She gave him a cock-eyed glance. "What's going on is I'm serving breakfast and you drank too much eggnog last night."

He wanted to remind her that she'd been pregnant only yesterday, but instinct told him he'd look more than foolish. Instead, he nodded and told Margot to play with the girls while he finished putting out the food. As he went between the living room and the kitchen, everything felt the same, exactly as it had the day before. Except now there were pictures on the walls of the new daughter, Tiffany. Suddenly he recalled her birth, how he'd sat in the waiting room with Roxie who couldn't wait to meet her new sister.

And yes, now he remembered—the complication.

The umbilical cord had been wrapped around baby Tiffany's neck. The nurses had told him it was as if Tiffany didn't want to come out of Margot's belly. He'd nearly lost them both. Thank God for the emergency C-section.

He poured Margot a cup of coffee and, when he brought it to her, thanked her for bringing the girls into the world. She laughed and said that he was surely hungover, but she appreciated the sentiment. They all ate a breakfast of toast, bacon, and eggs and, when finished, watched a movie together on the couch.

Halfway through the movie, Jason had forgotten about the apparent years he thought he'd lost. Holding his wife and children, he dozed off and dreamt he had fallen off a cliff, or maybe down a well—he wasn't sure, but the darkness seemed never-ending.

Suddenly he was in the hospital again, only this time Margot had lost the baby. A miscarriage. She wouldn't speak to him then or for weeks after. He tried to shower her with love and gifts and adventures, anything to take her mind off the baby, but the more he tried the more she hid away inside herself. He had wanted the child, too—more than anything—and he told her they could try again when she was ready. But she didn't want to. All she wanted to do was leave the home he worked so hard to give them and go for runs alone around Los Angeles. Until one day she came home and told him she'd found someone else, that she couldn't stop thinking about what they lost and that she was sorry but she had to move on. This someone else, a man whose face came to Jason more vividly than anything else in the dream. An image, a photo, or profile picture Jason must have burned into his retinas by staring at it for hours.

A man whose face shone so evidently through Roxie's.

He gasped and woke up. Margot and Roxie were gone, but Tiffany was still at his side. Only now she was bigger than earlier. Taller, and hair slightly longer. He looked around the room. The Christmas tree and all the toys had disappeared.

"What time is it?" he asked. "Where are your mother and sister?"

"The clock has four ones," Tiffany said. "It's been like that all day. And Mommy and Roxie went for a jog or something. I hate running. And you've been taking a nap, and I'm bored."

"Did your mother put away all the Christmas decorations while I was asleep?"

Tiffany looked up from a Rubik's Cube she'd been trying to solve.

"It hasn't been Christmas for a long time. Maybe you were just dreaming it was Christmas."

Jason tried to stand but his legs pricked from having sat on them too long. Tiffany looked at him askance. Her face was so familiar, yet so strange. This felt like only the second time he'd seen the child, but foggy memories of her life persisted to float to the top of his mind: Birthday parties. Scraped knees. Kite flying. Temper tantrums. The love he felt for her swelled inside him, yet it also felt misplaced, as if transplanted from someone else's heart.

"Do you remember anything from before you were born?" The question escaped him without prior thought. He nearly laughed at himself, so accusatory of an innocent child.

"I remember a lot of things," she said. "But it's hard to remember the time between after I died and before I was born."

After she died? She'd uttered the phrase so nonchalantly. He sat back down and put his arm around her, but she didn't look up from the cube. He asked her what she meant, told her in all seriousness that she had never died. She contested, all the while solving the cube with slow, meticulous turns. She told him about another world, one that existed before, yet at the same time as, this one. In this other world, she said, she had died and made it so they would go into a deep hole that never ended. Jason listened to her, without interrupting, as she spoke of being an adult, having her heart broken, and taking her life before committing one final act of revenge. She held out the cube for him to take. Each side was fixed to its correct color.

Jason was torn between punishing her for telling such a wild story and asking her to explain the logic between these separate worlds. Turning the cube in his hands, he thought about the dream. Margot leaving him. The face of her new suitor. Tiffany's story had much in common with his dream. If he had truly lost years of his life, he reasoned, maybe he had told Margot of his dreams before. Maybe Tiffany was rehashing a recurring nightmare she'd overheard him explaining to Margot.

Or maybe Tiffany wasn't making it up.

Wasn't there a possibility, even the slightest, that the loss of time was part and parcel of Tiffany's surreal imagination?

He decided to play along.

"How did you do it?" he asked. "I'm curious. The deep hole that never ends. The rift. The other world. I just don't understand how it's possible."

Tiffany smiled and held out her index finger above her head, as if to say, 'Eureka!'

"I wouldn't want to bore you with the science of it," she said. "But in the other life, I was a physicist. I figured out how to manipulate what they call dark matter. I had a lab and built a machine, and it was so strong that all the power went out in the whole city. The machine needed that much energy to make the rift. I didn't know if it was going to work, but before I died, I turned the machine on, and almost an entire year later, guess what? It worked! And I woke up here. But not only here. I woke up in other realities, too. And so did you. But don't worry. Before I died, I thought of a way for you all to go back to the other world if you wanted to. But I have to say, it won't be easy."

She told him about what he would have to do if he wanted to return to his old life, the sacrifice he would have to make. He wondered why he would want to return to that nightmare where Margot had left him, where they had lost a child, when he had everything and more right here. Here, Margot loved him. Here, his children brought him unconditional bliss. Tiffany assured him that, eventually, he would forget this conversation, that any memory of the other reality, even in dreams, would soon also vanish.

He watched Tiffany get a notebook and a box of crayons. As she drew a picture, he considered the unlikeliness of forgetting anything she had told him. Other realities? Another life? It was all too bizarre not to remember. Then again, he couldn't explain waking up from a night's sleep to find his second daughter had not only been born but was already old enough to talk. Or waking from a nap to find another year or so had passed without any inkling of where the time had gone. He put his arm around Tiffany and tried to suppress the oncoming headache while she drew, in all different shades of purple, a large snake coiled into a circle, devouring its tail.

They sat quietly for a long while, the creaks in the walls the only sounds other than their breathing and Tiffany's crayons against the paper. Jason grew transfixed by the picture, its colors reminding him—were they even memories?—of a coma-like numbness he'd recently fought. From where had the color violet come? For what reason did it trigger vertigo? He closed his eyes, breathed slowly, and tried to resist the swift onset of nausea.

It wasn't long before Jason heard a door open, followed by the cheerful voices of Margot and Roxie. When he opened his eyes, Tiffany had gone, but the picture of the snake remained where she sat. He was relieved to know that time had not again leaped forward. Roxie ran past him and into the bedroom, and when he stood, he saw Margot putting away groceries. Wearing a tank top and shorts, her hair in need of washing, she appeared to him more lovely than anything in this, or any other, world.

"Margot," he said, the sound more like a mantra to him than a name. "Margot, I love you so much."

Holding a gallon of milk, she turned to him and laughed. "If you love me so much, come in here and help me put all this away." He went into the kitchen, took the jug from her, and kissed her sweaty forehead. The taste of salt brought him back to waking on the beach when her belly was still plump with Tiffany, and Roxie had been so afraid of sisterhood. When he'd first caught the glimpse of the other man from his dream.

Putting away produce and canned goods, such a menial task, made Jason feel like time had finally slowed. He was somewhere he belonged. He heard his daughters playing in their bedroom, their giggling akin to a fresh fire crackling and warming him. His wife, whom he cherished above all others, stocked food in their shared home for their family and had not left him for another man.

As concrete as he wished these convictions would be, he couldn't deny that this façade, this wall of disillusionment, was mere rubble beneath his already-unsteady feet.

"Margot," he repeated. "Margot, tell me you'll never leave. No matter what happens. Tell me you're here to stay."

She rolled her eyes and sighed. "I'm gone for two hours and you're already worried about losing me again?" She stepped toward him, put her hand to his cheek. "How many times do I have to tell you? I'm here to stay. I'm not going anywhere. There's no one else. Never will be, never has been."

He wanted to tell her about the dream but realized he probably already had, sometime, somewhere, in the time he'd lost. But had the delusion of seeing another man's likeness in Roxie ever brought him to accuse Margot of cheating? Looking into her eyes, he saw a flicker of violet. The dream had been so vivid, Tiffany's story so specific to it, that he couldn't trust anymore what was real.

Never will be? Maybe.

Never has been? He couldn't believe it.

"I can't look at you without feeling betrayed," he said and removed himself from her touch. "I know I sound crazy, but something's not right. This is all too good to be true. I can't piece it together, and I can't deny the dreams."

"They're only dreams," she said, lowering her voice. "They're not real. Sometimes our dreams, our fears, can feel real, but they're just manifestations of our imagination."

"They're more than that to me. I think they're more than dreams. Here, look at this." He went to the couch and held up Tiffany's picture of the snake. "When I see this, it brings back all these thoughts and feelings. From another time, another place."

Margot took the picture and stared at it, squinting. "A little morbid, don't you think?"

Jason snatched the picture from her hands and went to the window, keeping his back to her. He looked out at Venice. The streets were quiet, unoccupied. Where was everyone? At a closer glance, he noticed there were no birds, no wind swaying the palm trees. Maybe it's an illusion, he thought. Maybe there's no life here.

Margot tried to calm him, suggested that he see a doctor. She said she would drive him, or they could get a babysitter and spend the night in a hotel, just to get away for a while. She put her hand on his shoulder. He shook her off, unwilling to accept that her love, her existence, was any more real than a life he fully remembered. A life that had supposedly never happened. She told him she was scared, that if he couldn't face her or listen to reason, she would take the girls and stay with a friend.

"Take them," he told her. "Take them to another man, whoever he is, and lock me out of your life for good."

His heart thumped. He couldn't recall such rage, such envy ever before pulsing so strongly through him. Facing her now, he gauged from her shocked expression how feral he must have appeared. She said nothing, went into the girls' room, and told them they were leaving, to gather their things. Jason heard Roxie ask Margot if he was coming. He couldn't bring himself to look at the child. "Daddy's got some things he has to do," Margot said. "We're going to go to a nice hotel for a couple of days where they have a pool, and we can go swimming."

Jason stood at the window and tried to slow his heart rate with deep breaths. He was being absurd. Childish. He knew that. But he couldn't let go of the fear that this life wasn't his life. And that speckle of violet in Margot's eye—had he imagined that, too? Or was it a sign, proof that whatever this was was a façade? He heard Margot and the girls behind him. "They want to say goodbye," Margot said. Jason felt his face twitch before he replaced his disgruntled visage with a smiling one. He knelt, opened his arms to his daughters, and cleared his throat to assuage any tears.

"You go and have fun," he said. "Be good for your mother."

Margot led Roxie and Tiffany by the hand, but once they were at the door, Tiffany ran back to him. She signaled for him to crouch down to her level and cupped her hands over her mouth, preparing to relay a secret. He knelt and put his ear to her hands. He felt her warm, sweet child's breath as she whispered, "Home. Home is wherever you want it to be."

She pulled away, smiled, and ran back over to Margot and Roxie. Jason stood and watched them go through the front door. "This is not goodbye," he said. Margot didn't flinch at the words. Once the door was closed, he exhaled, felt the emptiness inside him, inside the house. He went to the window and saw the three of them—his girls—get in the car and drive off. As the car turned out of view, he looked around again for any sign of life, anything to make him feel less alone in this world, this reality, whatever this place was where he couldn't trust the linear progression of time.

There was nothing but his own reflection in the glass. He picked up Tiffany's drawing of the violet snake eating itself. Carrying the picture, his gaze locked on it, he walked through each room of the house. He thought that maybe the picture, if he read it correctly, would guide him like a map to the door to the other world. The door to his other life. His real home.

Maybe if I return to the beach, he thought, I'll find the rift that brought me here. But it was so long ago, he realized, that he'd first come through and found himself in this new place. As Tiffany had said, there was only one way to go back. He remembered the pain of waiting for her to be born.

She'd told him he would have to make a sacrifice.

When he looked up from Tiffany's drawing he realized he'd been standing in his daughters' room. The paper fell from his fingertips and swished to the floor. The snake stared up at him. He sat down on Tiffany's bed and prepared himself for what he had to do.

Dear Jason,

What a delight it was to find you.

Another show of the universe throwing curveballs.

When we first encountered, my mind was still sluggish.

It wasn't until you asked me what I remembered before I was born that everything from before the rift came flooding back.

I was able to experience memories from multiple realities. I remembered a death. I remembered a pained birth. The memories were mine, yet they were not my own. I tried to explain the black hole to you, but my adult mind was wrestling against a child's mouth. I saw myself coming into this world; I saw myself going out; both times a coil around my neck.

How could anyone possibly explain that?

Yet the more I tried to explain, the easier you seemed to understand. You were so willing to trust, which proves to be one of your constants.

I drew for you the ouroboros. And I could tell from your expression that your memories had begun to return. Margot came home and you wanted to embrace your second chance with her. Yet you couldn't let go of the betrayal ensnaring you like a fishhook.

When I witnessed your pain, it was so refreshing to know I no longer had to feel alone in my suffering.

You had suffered from Margot what I had suffered from Knox.

Before the rift, I blamed myself. I blamed Knox. I blamed Margot. We had all caused each other suffering. But you, Jason—I fear you are the one in this narrative who remains blameless. What suffering did you instill? I learned of the loss you and Margot shared—a loss that is a constant in the ouroboros of our story together.

You, Jason, might be the best of us.

Which is why I wanted you to find your home.

No, that isn't entirely accurate.

I wanted you to choose your home.

Whichever reality that may be.

28

On the drive back to the house, Margot played an old Janis Joplin album for the girls, to which they knew all the words. While they sang in the back seat, Margot thought of their father's face, though she could not yet, try as she might, remember his name. She pulled into the driveway and let out the girls, who kept asking her questions: What's for dinner? Can we watch a movie tonight? Can we have dessert? What's your favorite ice cream flavor, Mommy? She gave them the same stock answer she'd use whenever she couldn't collect her thoughts: It's a surprise. Since their father died, she could now recall, she'd been the only one, other than each other, with whom the girls could converse. Needless to say, it was tiring being their sole source of comfort. In whom did she have to find comfort? The girls were there for her, sure, but it was not right for a mother to share with her children such misery. And so, she kept it all locked tightly within herself—the mystery, the guilt, the confusion, the grief, the splicing urge to scream, the frigidness of loss, the resentment surrounding her husband's reasons for taking his own life.

Inside the house, she made the girls a frozen pizza and turned on the television to occupy them while she went into her bedroom to look through old pictures. On the way into her room, she had to pass the girls'. They always kept the door closed, now; they didn't go in there anymore. Margot thought of that room like a tomb, a crypt, a mausoleum. She feared opening the door would release his ghost or, worse, that she'd find his body in there again and be forced to relive the whole thing.

She closed the door to her bedroom and retrieved a shoebox from the closet. Though the image of her daughters' father's face had started to return to the forefront of her mind, she needed something to jog her memory. Sitting on the bed, she placed the shoebox lid beside her and looked down into the pile of ephemera. Photographs, notes, ticket stubs, pamphlets—fragments collected over time that formed but a jagged portrait of the man she loved and the life they lived. She lifted an old Polaroid from the box, held it at a distance from her face. Too much proximity, she knew, would make the memories resurface too quickly.

As her eyes focused on the man's face, she felt hairs rise on the nape of her neck. Written below the image, in the polaroid's white space, was his name:

Jason.

She remembered moving from Florida to California with him, the road trip during which they stopped at all the major cities. In the shoebox, she had photos for every one of them: Her and Jason sharing a po'boy in New Orleans. Jason passed out in a Lafayette hotel room. A photo Jason had taken of her at a rest stop bathroom in Nowhere, Texas, her hand blocking her face, panties around her ankles. Back then, she never expected they'd have two daughters. She and Jason had talked what seemed incessantly about the luck, the gift that had been their children. Jason loved them with every mote of his being—she knew that. So, what had pushed him to make that irrevocable decision? To her knowledge—and she'd been somewhat of an authority on Jason—he'd never battled with depression. Never once spoke about inner pain, never shown any signs of turmoil or distress. Not until that last day.

She should have known not to leave when he told her about the dreams that seemed like more than dreams. Why had he felt so betrayed? She often sifted through the pile in the shoebox, hoping to magically find a parting note from him. Although there had been nothing near him other than Tiffany's drawing, Margot often wondered if she'd missed something. That maybe Jason had hidden a letter to her amidst the mounds of papers she'd for years meant to compile into a scrapbook. Something to remember him by. Something to ease her woes.

But no.

Nothing, save Tiffany's bizarre drawing. Margot took it out of the box and unfolded it. A purple snake eating its tail. Brighter than purple. Violet. The drawing was a little grotesque, sure—but Margot couldn't deny Tiffany's artistic sensibilities. Roxie, on the other hand, took after her father. She was practical. Analytical, even. But Tiffany? She was no doubt an artist's daughter. Margot looked at the precision of Tiffany's lines, the balance of the zen-like circle. The eye of the snake seemed to hook Margot, pushed her to drift into the open waters of thought. She wondered if this had been the last thing Jason saw. A moment of darkness befell her—the darkness she imagined had consumed Jason. The darkness of his last living seconds. The darkness of his first non-living seconds. She felt it deep within her. She closed her eyes but sensed the lingering gaze of the snake upon her. The sounds of the room faded, as did the sound of her children's laughter.

There was stillness.

Movement—the rush of falling. Falling, and yet never colliding with the inevitable earth.

There was a face.

A man's face.

Jason's?

No.

Another's.

Remnant of the stranger she'd barely remembered at the beach when she questioned Roxie about her father. A semblance in her firstborn she couldn't place.

As she lingered on this face in her mind's eye, the truth began to slowly unravel: When Jason had accused her of seeing another man, when he had told her about the dreams, she didn't want to tell him that she'd had similar visions. This new man's face had appeared to her in dreams back then, too. But never had she linked this man to Roxie. Maybe Jason wouldn't have done it if she'd confessed to the dreams, or to doing something she didn't—would never—do.

It's not your fault.

A voice—the new man's. Familiar, calming.

At first, his face was out of focus, but the longer she kept it centered in her mind, the clearer it slowly became. Images began to superimpose over the darkness: A canyon. A chapel. A dog. A balcony. An earthquake. This man was beside her in each passing image. A part of her life, a hinge upon which the door of her memories opened and closed.

And where had Jason been in these memories?

It was as if these faux experiences were specifically devoid of him. It was as if they were from another time.

Another place.

"Mommy?"

Margot opened her eyes. Tiffany stood beside her, a puzzled look on her face. Margot quickly folded the drawing, put it back in the shoebox, and closed it.

"Yes, darling?"

"What are you doing?"

Margot felt the irk of being questioned. Couldn't she just get a moment of peace without having to explain herself?

"I could ask you the same thing. You know not to come into Mommy's room when the door's closed."

Tiffany's face went from puzzled to pouty.

"But Roxie fell asleep on the couch and I'm bored and I missed you and now I miss Daddy." Her little hands went for the shoebox, but Margot pulled it out of reach.

"Stop it," Margot said. "Before you ruin something."

Tiffany cocked her head, unexpectant of such an offense. Margot saw her lower lip tremble, eyes swelling. She wondered what had caused her to say that.

I must be a shitty mother to spite my own daughter, she thought.

"Come here," she said, taking Tiffany into her arms. "Momma's sorry. I was mean. You can go through the box. I know you miss your father. I miss him, too."

Tiffany looked up, her eyes red with tears.

"You don't have to be sorry," she said. "I should be sorry. It's all my fault."

"No, it's not," Margot said. She put her hands on Tiffany's hot cheeks. "Your father made that choice all by himself. It's no one's fault. Do not blame yourself for that, do you understand?"

Tiffany ran her hand across a streak of Margot's hair.

"That's not what I meant," she said. "I mean what I told you at the beach."

Margot remembered what Tiffany said about the earthquake, the hole in the ground, the other life. She pushed the girl's hand away.

"I don't want to hear any more nonsense," Margot said. She considered if the trait that had pushed Jason into madness could have been inherited.

But what of her madness?

"But it's not nonsense," Tiffany said. "You have to listen. I know it's hard to believe me. But I want you to understand what Daddy understood."

Margot resented her for speaking, as though this animosity had been boiling for a lifetime. She had to stop herself from telling the child to shut her mouth.

"Tell me," Margot said. "What did Daddy understand?"

Tiffany ceased her sniffling; she must have taken heed of the scorn in Margot's voice.

"He understood that this place is only real if you want it to be," she said. "He understood that all of this was like an illusion. And that's what you need to see, Mommy. You need to think back to before. You have me and Roxie now, but that's only because in the other life you almost had two babies. You lost the first one with Daddy before it was born. And the second one was with another man." Tiffany paused, looked over toward the living room, and back again. "You would have had that baby if you didn't go into the rift to come here."

Margot stood from the bed, nearly knocking the girl down. The ephemera from the shoebox was scattered across the floor. Images of Jason and the girls stared up at her from the photographs. She dug her fingernails into her palms, restrained herself from striking Tiffany.

"You're being a little shit," she said, and immediately clasped her hand over her mouth.

She'd been half-conscious when the obstetrician pulled Tiffany from her. Her umbilical cord had been wrapped around her baby's neck. Even in that state of minimal awareness, Margot prayed for God to spare her child. Looking at Tiffany now, Margot remembered clutching the frame of the hospital bed when she'd had a vision of her daughter as a grown woman, hanging by her neck from a rope. Before she'd realized it, the nurse had placed the baby in her arms. Margot had run her fingers along the tender neck of the screaming child and proclaimed her "Tiffany."

"I don't want to make you upset," Tiffany said. "I just want you to know the truth, that you have what you lost." The girl took a slow step forward. "That's what Daddy knew. But he didn't want it." She bent down, picked up a photo of Jason and Roxie, and held it for Margot to see. "In the other life, you chose someone else. And if you close your eyes and think hard, I know you'll remember him."

Slow to let her eyes settle on the photo, Margot could not deny the great divide between their features. No, Roxie's were that of another's.

The other man. Margot envisioned his face again, a split second.

How could Tiffany know?

"He was yours," Tiffany said, "after he was mine."

Margot noticed a scowl on the girl's face, a tinge of resentment.

"He chose you. And I don't know why. And that's why we're here. Because you took him from me. You took away what I loved, what made me happy. I thought I would have a family. A baby. With him. He—" again she looked toward the living room where Roxie lay asleep. "He loved me."

Tiffany's breathing had grown rapid. Margot sensed that the girl had been waiting a long time to say these things. Though, how could she be so impassioned by someone who didn't even exist?

If Tiffany could be so affected by the mere mention of him, and Margot could visualize his face, then somehow, somewhere, sometime, the man and their connection to him must have been real.

"Tell me more," Margot said.

Tiffany furled an eyebrow. "You can't unlearn what I tell you."

Margot nodded. Tiffany started to pick up the mess of photos and notes from the floor.

"You can keep everything that's here," Tiffany said. "In time you will forget the other life. You won't be able to picture the other man's face anymore. Not even when you look at Roxie." She gave Margot an all-knowing glance. Had her deepest thoughts been that transparent? "But you have us. You have your children.

"I made it so that you can have this life or the other one. In the other life, I died. I can't go back there again. I did it to myself. And when I came to this life, my neck was still caught. But it was caught in you. In your body.

"I wanted to get away from you, and the pain you caused me, so badly. But it just goes to show we can never escape the past. It doesn't matter if it's this life, or the one before it, or the one after it. We keep going around and around, loving and hurting and running. It never stops. Not for me, or you, or anyone.

"And I realized I can never escape you, that you're as much a part of me as myself, anything I see or think or feel or perceive. The four of us are bound together, it seems."

She looked at a picture of Jason and Roxie in her hands.

"Daddy—Jason—knew that in the other life you didn't choose him. He couldn't accept that you would choose him here. So, he went back, even though he loves you and could have had you here. That's why I wanted him to come through the rift, too. He and I both lost who we love because they no longer loved us. Not in the way that we still loved them. But he was stronger than I was. He didn't do anything he couldn't undo. I sent the little girl to him because he had been waiting so long for you. I planned for the power to go out, and for you and Knox to have nowhere to go."

Knox.

The other man. Hearing the name crystallized the blurred face in Margot's mind.

Knox—the man she married.

The man whose child she carried before coming here.

"I must go back," Margot said. "What do I do?"

"It will take a sacrifice," Tiffany said. "You have to do what I did to get here." She held up the photograph so that Jason's smiling face appeared to stare at Margot. "What he did to go back."

Margot felt the twist in her gut. Now she remembered Knox, a phone call, his incomprehensible sobs. Margot had instantly felt responsible for ruining Knox's life and Tiffany's. She remembered thinking that if she'd never gone for a jog at Runyon Canyon and met Knox, if she'd never miscarried and felt the need to separate from Jason, maybe Tiffany would have still been alive. She remembered the months of guilt and dark, monochromatic abstracts she'd painted in hopes of relieving the grief. The constant wondering if Knox had only stayed with her as a testament to his own choice, to prove to himself that Tiffany had not died for nothing. Over a year, and still, Margot was not over the insecurities. But she had learned to accept them when she realized she was pregnant again.

Margot took the photo of Jason and Roxie from Tiffany's fingers. She looked into Tiffany's eyes, tinted like brilliant amethysts. Neither this daughter nor the other daughter—Roxana—was truly hers. She could allow herself to forget it all, as Tiffany had assured, and go on loving them—but right now she knew that her real child, the one yet to be born, was waiting for her, in her belly, on the other side.

She knelt, kissed Tiffany on the forehead, and asked her to wait in the living room with her sister.

29

KNOX STOOD OVER his daughter—Margot—and wondered if he would be able to leave her. She lay with her eyes closed and blankets pulled up to her chin, snoring sweetly in the quiet of the bedroom. He put his finger to her soft cheek, though she didn't so much as shift at his touch. Sound asleep, his daughter. This person, his heart. He stared at her little face; it was so serene in the violet light. Flashes of the Margot from the other reality—his reality—perforated his thoughts: Margot painting, Margot cooking, Margot walking the dog. Every image—memory?—of her appeared blurred in his mind, as though filmed without the camera lens focused. He tried to force her face into focus, to summon a clear representation to compare with the sleeping child. Their likeness, despite his fuzzy recollection, couldn't be denied.

His finger began to tremble, a sharp pain spliced across his head. He winced, pulled his hand away, and put it to his face. Warmth from his nose, above his lip. He touched the area—wet. On his fingertips, blood darker than crimson in the violet light.

He left the room, the light, the girl, and he asked Tiffany what was happening to him. She told him there was now a rift in his mind, in his heart, that would soon close. She said his memories from before fought with the creation of memories in the present. The overlap, she said, took a physical toll on the body. She told him to sit down and, after he did, she cleaned the blood with a damp washrag. The warm rag felt good against his face; it felt like love. He looked into Tiffany's eyes, her face nearly identical to how it had been before she died. He peered down at her hands and cautiously reached to hold them. The feeling of her fingers and knuckles—so different from Margot's—made him think back to his last moment with her.

Tiffany had been sitting on the balcony at The Libra with Lane's head in her lap and listening to Bach. Knox had come home with the intent of telling Tiffany everything, but when he found her smoking a cigarette—something she never did—he figured she already knew.

"Six years," Tiffany had said after taking a deep, slow drag. The smoke exited her nostrils, enough to make Lane get up and go inside, head limp as he brushed past Knox. "I gave you six years of my life. Did it mean nothing?"

He tried to sit beside her, but she raised her hand to halt him.

"How did you find out?"

"Your online messages," she said. "I logged into your account."

He leaned against the balcony's ledge and watched traffic build along Hollywood Boulevard. With Tiffany at his back, he felt the sting of shame rise into his throat. His fingernails dug into the ledge, and he regretted moving across the country with her only to break her heart and betray her.

"Do you love her?"

He dug his nails deeper into the ledge.

"Please answer me."

I love you both, he wanted to say. I am a person torn between the past and the future. I love what we have been, yet I love what I might become with her.

"I think I do," he said. "And, I know this isn't what you want to hear, but I haven't exactly stopped loving you. It's complicated, Tiffany."

He turned around and saw her stubbing the cigarette on the upholstery. She was shaking her head. She was crying. He tried to reach out to grab her hand, but she flinched away, grabbed her keys, and got up to leave. He called her name, but she didn't stop.

The last he saw of her alive was her walking out the door, her face slightly angled toward him while she shut it behind her, her eyes purposefully turned away from him.

Knox looked up from her hands in his. She asked him if he was going to stay with her this time. He brought her hands to his lips, the warmth of her flesh calming, inviting. So familiar were her hands. So many times before had he cherished their elegance. He kissed the tips of her fingers and shook his head.

"You know I can't," he said. "I loved you deeply, but this place doesn't justify the choices we made. My heart is with Margot. My Margot. And our baby. What is done cannot be undone."

She put her hand to his cheek.

She said, "We were happy. I remember joy. I remember adventure. The uncertainty of the future wasn't as scary, knowing I had you. Your love gave me the courage to face the wild unknown. The unknown is what brought us together. It only makes sense that it is also what takes us apart."

She smiled, pulled her hand away, and turned toward Margot's room. "I'm going to take her somewhere now, while she's fast asleep. If you're going to return, it's best to do it now, before the memories fade. No good can come of delaying the inevitable."

She stood and started for the girl's room, but Knox took her hand one last time.

"Will I remember any of this? Will I remember you?"

She squeezed his fingers and released herself from him.

"I don't know," she said. "I didn't think that far ahead with this experiment. I thought for sure I wouldn't lose you again."

Another quick smile and she disappeared into the girl's room. She came out with the girl draped over her shoulder.

"Maybe this is finally goodbye," she whispered. Knox noticed how carefully Tiffany held the girl, how natural the role of mother fit her. He wondered if they would still be in this reality once he was gone, if he'd be abandoning one family for another, leaving them alone just as Tiffany had done in the other life. Suddenly, visions of their daughter's birth streamed to the forefront of his mind—Tiffany in the hospital bed, her vice-strong grip nearly enough to break his hand, the sound of her screams bringing him both guilt for the pain he'd caused her and pleasure for the life he'd helped create. The sight of the baby still tethered to Tiffany. The elation he felt when the doctor placed the baby in his arms, and when he put the baby into Tiffany's. He questioned, staring at Tiffany now holding a grown version of that baby, how those memories could be both real and not. He questioned how the history of these three people could be erased, could be abandoned.

He felt the need to get up and embrace them, but Tiffany gestured for him to keep distant.

"We shouldn't make it harder than it has to be," she said. "I want you to go into her room and shut the door.

We'll be gone in a few moments. Listen for the front door to shut, and, when you're ready, you can do what is necessary."

He said, "Can't you come with me? Can't you return, too?"

She smiled. "We can't forget Persephone's warning to Orpheus."

He nodded. "For if before he reaches the realms of air..."

She said, "He backward cast his eyes to view the fair..."

"The forfeit grant, that instant, the void is made..."

"And she forever left a lifeless shade."

He shunted his eyes and started for the bedroom. He fought the impulse to hold Tiffany and their daughter one last time. With the glow of the violet nightlight cast upon their faces, Knox resisted the pull toward them and stepped into the light's source. He closed the bedroom door behind him and pressed his palm against the wood. His breathing heavy, he tuned out the drumming of his heart to listen for Tiffany and Margot's exit. When he heard the front door close and lock, he backed away from the door and looked around the room. Every toy, poster, book, and knick-knack in the room was enveloped in the violet light. Even his hands, as he held them up to his face, looked alien in the glow of the nightlight. Without his daughter in the room, the space felt cold, hollow. It felt lifeless, even though his pulse and breathing proved otherwise.

Now alone, Knox had to think of how to do it. He knew the longer he spent in his daughter's room, the harder it would be to convince himself to leave. He scanned the room in search of an idea, an object—anything to spark his imagination. How had Tiffany chosen her method?

The purest way to do it, he remembered. *The coil of unbecoming death*. He remembered the words, yet it was also like he'd experienced them for the first time. He realized that all of life, in its recursive stream of thoughts and experiences and memories, was akin to the anomaly of déjà vu; to see again, to relive a moment or incident that should be new, yet somehow feels familiar. Was it that search for newness that made him first choose Margot over Tiffany? Was it the desire to retain the familiarity of life that made him choose her again this time? Quickly, he opened the bedroom door and went to the closet where Tiffany had earlier been hiding. He felt again the chill of recollection, the dredging of unwanted memories.

There was a beam in the closet's ceiling.

A ligature point that would hold him.

My price to pay, he thought.

To feel what she felt.

He gathered the materials—the rope and chair—and turned out all the lights in the house. The last light was the violet nightlight in Margot's room. He unplugged it and embraced the complete darkness.

The light fell fast.

First, it broke through the slit under the closet door, as if the California sunshine had come to seize him. Then the light engulfed the entire closet; it ate the darkness around him. Then the light entered him. It infiltrated his eyes and his mouth and all other orifices until the light consumed him and he became the light.

The absence of darkness, light.

The inverse of violet, yellow.

Yellow, his daughter. A girl alive, a girl not yet born.

Citrine, his wife. A woman vanquished, a woman ripe with life.

Amber, his past. A mistake fossilized, a mistake jeweled.

Gold, his life. A gift forsaken, a gift embraced.

The light began to pull at the body and all that was once flesh and bone and blood evaporated, transcended beyond the building and the city until the sky's periphery, the all-seeing earthly gaze, became the only point of view. Anything that had been body or mind or soul ceased to be and there was now gravity. There was the sky reflecting ocean and there was fire beyond that. From the fire came luminance and all that had ever been was born of that luminance. All that had ever been and all versions of their being.

And from where had the absence of light come?

Nightfall.

Ceaselessness.

Death.

All which exists is only another form of that which exists not.

Knox smelled salt and felt hot, coarse sand against his skin. He opened his eyes, but the light was too bright to keep them open. He heard the cry of gulls and the soft roll of waves against the shore. From the distance came the sound of voices and music, both amplified and echoing around him.

"Come one, come all," said a voice over a loudspeaker. "See the woman with two heads and two hearts! See the sawed-in-half man! See the dead come back to life!"

With his fingers in the sand, Knox remembered having heard before the Freakshow's invitation. He and Tiffany had ventured down the Venice Beach boardwalk dozens of times, always laughing at the bizarre lineup. He'd thought it equally bizarre how fascinated she was by the oddities and anomalies. "Defiant of physics," she'd once said before dragging him in to watch a woman swallow a sword.

As his eyes adjusted to the sunlight, he was able to bring himself to his feet. The beach dwellers surrounding him played Frisbee, splashed around in the nearby water, and sunbathed with books at hand. He looked around for Tiffany, though he hadn't quite regained his balance. His mouth was dry when he tried to say her name. He staggered with each step and wondered how he'd gotten to the beach, let alone how he woke up there. The overlapping sounds of music and hundreds of conversations disoriented him as he slowly made his way from the shoreline to the boardwalk. A pain throbbed in his head; his neck felt sore as if whiplashed.

Where was Tiffany? He tried to think of the last time he saw her. He envisioned her in a house, holding a child, saying goodbye.

But that couldn't be right. They didn't know anybody with children. He patted his pockets for his phone, but it wasn't there. He spun around and called out Tiffany's name. A pair of teenagers playing Frisbee looked at him funny. He kept walking toward the boardwalk, and the sound of a dog barking caught his attention.

It was a few yards away and appeared to be barking at him. A Golden Lab tied to a signpost.

Lane.

Knox ran over to the dog and, once he was within reach, the dog whined and pounced toward him, practically choking itself with the taut leash.

"Whoa, boy." Knox knelt to caress the dog's fur. It licked his fingers rapidly, barely able to contain itself.

"What kind of asshole leaves a dog tied up for hours at a time?"

Knox looked up to see a young woman smoking a cigarette.

"You're lucky I didn't call animal control, man. That's cruelty." She exhaled and flicked the butt into the sand near Knox before burying it with her shoe.

"I'm sorry," he said. "Thank you." Hours at a time? How long had he been asleep in the sand?

And where was Tiffany?

"No need to say sorry to me, man," the woman said. "The dog's the one who deserves an apology." She walked off and disappeared into the crowd. Knox felt Lane's cold nose against his face and a slow, slobbery lick. He looked into the dog's pouty eyes and felt guilt stirring in his stomach.

But something wasn't right. He and Tiffany would never neglect their dog. He reached to untie the leash from the signpost when a glimmer of gold caught his eye. A ring hung from Lane's collar. A wedding band.

Had Tiffany left it for him?

He unfastened the collar and let the ring drop into his palm. He held it up to the light, looked through the hole.

A mysterious beach proposal?

No, Tiffany wouldn't have done that.

He felt the leash tighten. Lane was trying to pull him away from the boardwalk and toward the beach. Knox quickly slid the ring onto his finger, a perfect fit, and followed the dog. With his nose to the sand, Lane guided Knox in the direction of the Santa Monica Mountains. Sniffing rapidly and zigzagging, the dog was on a mission—a hunt. Knox picked up his speed, nearly jogging to keep up with Lane, who had no concern for the people sunbathing or building sandcastles.

After what Knox estimated to be half a mile, Lane stopped next to a man who sat in the sand with arms wrapped around bent knees. The man stared at the ocean, seemingly detached from the world until Lane woofed at him. The man turned his head, more so looking beyond them than at them. Knox tried to escape the man's distant gaze, but Lane wouldn't budge.

"Who are you?" said the man.

"Sorry," Knox said. "My dog, he—"

Before Knox could say any more, he realized he had somewhere before seen this man. As Knox tried to recall the time or the place, the man's expression changed from stagnant to dismayed.

"You're him," the man said. "But I don't understand. A moment ago, I had it all. Everything I lost and more. But I didn't want it. I couldn't keep it, knowing that she chose you."

Knox could sense what was going on behind the man's wild eyes, a skirmish of thoughts. Knox felt it, too. Of course, at first, the only woman Knox imagined the man referring to was Tiffany, but as a briny gust of wind skimmed his face, he had the sudden intimation that Tiffany was gone. He heard the cry of the gulls and felt the vibrations of her voice in their echoes across the shore. He tasted the salt of her kiss coming off the ocean's breeze. A clear blue sky; vacuity in the pit of his stomach.

There was no doubt in his mind.

There was no longer a Tiffany but the one in his memory.

The man got to his feet, brushed the sand from his clothes, and looked from Lane to Knox. "I can tell you don't remember," he said. "That's okay. I barely can, either. But it will come back to you soon, and in pieces."

The hairs on Knox's arms and neck rose. He and the man looked into each other's eyes, and Knox pictured the face of another woman. He couldn't quite make out her features, only her likeness. A pain throbbed in his head as he tried to summon a clear vision of the woman's face.

But the more of the new woman's face that crystallized in his mind, the less he remembered of Tiffany's.

Who was she, and why had she chosen him over this man?

"Tell me about her," Knox said. "Tell me who she is. Where I can find her."

The man raised his hand and put it on Knox's shoulder.

He said, "There's nothing I can tell you that you don't already know." He gave Knox's shoulder a gentle squeeze, lowered his hand to pet Lane, and pursed his lips. With a hesitant grin, he turned toward the boardwalk and crossed the sand until immersed in the swarm of people, no longer in Knox's line of sight.

Lane woofed quietly and nudged Knox's hand with his head. Knox patted the dog and looked at the ring on his finger. It glistened in the sunlight, this artifact that must have tied him to the woman whose face he longed to look upon, whose name he could not recall.

K.,

For us, love will always be a constant.

I must believe that.

Even after you betrayed me, I must believe that you still loved me.

Why else would our various incarnations have been built upon relationships of love? I couldn't imagine what it would have been like for you to love me as a child and then to feel the echoes of another kind of love. I told you there was a rift in your mind and heart that would soon close because I couldn't accept the way our love had manifested.[∞] *I knew if you had a choice, you wouldn't be able to accept it either. Once the rift*

[∞] Love, as we know it in the English language, can be quite vague. In Greek, on the other hand, there are multiple ways to identify love. If there is a God, one might suppose the kind of love He has for us is unconditional, self-sacrificing, or *Agape*. The kind of love we shared for six years would be *Eros*, or romantic love. The kind of love we seemed to have inherited in this incarnation would be *Storge*, or the love of family, as in the parent and child relationship.

in your mind closed, there would no longer be a choice for you. You might not have understood this, but the only way to potentially recalibrate our Coils, to straighten out our timelines, was to close the rift within the minds of each party.

I know now that loving her was not a choice. It was your destiny. Right now—somewhere out there—there is another version of me writing another version of this letter for another reason. Or perhaps Margot is the one writing you a letter. I'm certain there are also numerous versions in which you are the one writing the letter, K. Versions in which you were not the betrayer but the betrayed. It is this truth—our infinite versions—that has taught me how significant we all are in each go-around.

We have gone into our respective underworlds. We have found a way around the point of no return. But at a cost. And in our ways, we have all looked back; we have all, in some incarnation, lost something to the darkness.

30

MARGOT HAD RETURNED to the darkness and the light, and her eyes were opening slowly, as if for the first time. She heard waves breaking nearby, and she felt hot sunrays beaming onto her body. She thought she was at Vero Beach, waiting for Jason to return from his surf. How long had she been asleep? Fragments of a dream—perhaps a nightmare—lingered in her head: a cavernous pit, an earthquake, a line of bodies covered by a tarpaulin in the street. She assumed these images had come from a film she'd recently seen, though she couldn't quite remember.

She shielded her eyes from the bright sunlight with her hands and instantly felt dizzy, disoriented. She couldn't tell if she was facing east or west, the pull of vertigo so strong she had to steady herself with her hands, like a tripod in the sand. That's when the first twinge of pain shot through her belly, strong enough to make her wail.

"Are you okay?"

A shadow suddenly loomed over her, brought by a figure blocking the sun. Margot thought it was Jason until she saw that the figure was holding a leash, his dog—a Golden Lab—whining at, and now licking, Margot.

"Some kind of pain," she said. "Not sure why."

The figure knelt and put his hand on her back. She shrugged, put off by how forward he and his dog were.

"Just trying to help," he said.

"Your dog," she said.

"He must like you."

Margot couldn't help but reach and stroke the dog's fur. The man looked at her hand and held up his own next to it.

"Weird," he said. "Our rings. They're practically identical."

Margot hadn't even noticed the ring. She drew her hand back and examined it closely. A wedding band, more flush around her finger than she'd have liked.

Had she and Jason—?

No. It was coming back to her now. He'd asked her, but she couldn't bear it after what they lost.

She looked around the beach for him and realized how far she was from Vero. On the exact opposite side of the country. Behind her was the boardwalk where she'd once sold her paintings beneath a canopy, and there was the small shop where she and Jason had often stopped for gyros and French fries. California, she remembered, was her home now.

California, with its rainless summers.

Los Angeles, with its endless opportunities.

Everything had changed, and, for the life of her, she couldn't piece together the moments that had brought her to this one. Jason, and her history with him, was no longer a part of her present. This much had come rushing back to her. But what of this ring? She had half a mind to remove it and cast it into the sand—but something stopped her. Bereft of the reason for her attachment to this object, she grabbed the man's hand and compared his ring to hers. Simple, with a thin lip embellishing the outer edges. Still gripping his hand, she looked upon his face in search of any mal intent, sensing the interrogative expression forming upon her face.

"Is this some kind of joke?" she said. "Did you slip this on my finger while I was passed out?"

He withdrew his hand from hers and pulled the dog's leash so it would retract some of its affection toward her.

"Sorry I bothered you," he said. He started to rise, but something caused Margot to grab him by the bottom of his shirt. In that instant, with the cloth of his shirt in her clutches, she realized how absent were her memories, how severed was her experience—there was no linchpin to connect her to what had brought her to this beach and this man and his curiously loving dog.

With the second surge of pain that shot through her belly and uterus, she gripped the man's shirt tighter to steady herself, pulling him to his knees. Her face contorted from the pain—even the dog could sense it, its whimpers oddly comforting as she dug her other hand into the sand.

"Something's wrong," she said to the man, his face now inches from hers, her fingers clutching his shirt collar. He stared at the sand under her legs.

"We've got to get you to a hospital," he said.

She now felt the warmth and wetness beneath her legs. Had she pissed herself?

She looked down and saw—how had she possibly missed it?—her bulging stomach. A pregnant belly.

"I can't—"

"Your water," the man said. "Got to go. Now."

As he surveyed the beach, she felt her heart rate increase, the panic rising. It was as though she had awoken in someone else's life, another woman's body. The man's hands were under her arm, now, trying to bring her to her feet. He spoke to her, something about not being able to leave her there alone. The sudden weight of her belly threw her off balance, but the man caught her before she fell over. With one hand on her shoulder and the other on her stomach, she noticed a familiarity in his gentle touch.

"I'm scared," she said, the words escaping seemingly against her will.

"I won't let anything happen to you." Looking into his eyes, she believed him and yielded to the way he steered her, incrementally, toward the boardwalk. Together, they lumbered across the sand and ignored the gazes and comments of onlookers. The dog kept to her side as though it were her guardian. A thought crept into her mind, a vision of the beach, the same beach, but somehow different. She envisioned a crater and a little girl jumping into it. A man came running after the girl, followed by a second man. There was nobody else around, and she feared what would happen if either man went in after the girl. When she snapped out of the vision, she looked around and wondered how it could be that this imaginary version of the beach existed in tandem with the one in front of her.

But then again, how could she have possibly forgotten the fact that she was nine months pregnant, mere moments from going into labor? She wondered if the other beach, with its gaping fissure and disappeared girl, could be the real world, rendering this one a dream, an illusion.

Once she and the man reached the pavement, it seemed that his level of panic had escalated beyond even hers. He jumped up and down, peering over the heads of tourists and locals. She saw him think to check his pockets for his phone, which was not there. Hers, too, was gone—she didn't even have a purse with her when she woke up. The dog looked from her to him and barked when the man started jumping again.

"What are you looking for?" she said.

"Help," he said. "Nearest hospital or doctor."

She took deep, slow breaths to calm herself. Her back felt hardened, and she grew dizzy at the thought of a baby pressing against her nerves.

"Marina Del Rey," she said. "That's the nearest hospital." She remembered getting her first ultrasound there, and the surgery that followed weeks after. With the thought of losing her first child, another memory returned, more recent—a home pregnancy test in a bathroom garbage can.

An apartment in Hollywood.

An earthquake.

"That's about three miles," the man said.

"Do you have a car?" She didn't need a response to know the answer.

"Wait here," he said.

He started to turn and run but she took him by the wrist.

"You can't leave me here like this."

"I'm not leaving you," he said. "Here, take him."

He handed her the leash.

"What's his name?"

"Lane," he said. "I'm Knox."

"Margot."

"I'll be right back, Margot. I think I know someone who can help."

She watched him run until he was no longer in her field of vision. The dog planted itself at her side, looked up at her with its tongue out, its tail slapping the concrete.

"Good boy," she said. "Lane."

More hesitant she was to say the man's name, until, like a bubble rising through water, it emerged from her mouth.

31

Jason was about to turn down Windward Circle when he heard someone shouting. He did not think to look, considering the regular amount of fairly crazy people who meandered Venice on a given day. From the intersection, with the beach now far behind him, he saw his house and felt eager to return, clean it up, and maybe put it back on the market. Though it had taken over a year, he no longer felt bound to Los Angeles and the prospects about which he'd once fantasized. Without Margot, there was nothing for him here other than a high-paying job at CavumCorp. He remembered finding the little gray-eyed girl and speaking, on the other side, with his daughter—Tiffany—the same name as Margot's husband's ex. Even though the girl he'd found near the statue of Thoth had resembled Margot, he wondered if she and Tiffany were the same. Did the girl, too, have to make the ultimate sacrifice before arriving to him? He wondered if these memories were even real, or if he'd long lost his mind. With a closer look he saw—could it be?—the statue of Thoth was no longer erected in the middle of the Circle. There was no statue at all.

The shouting grew closer, someone yelling, "Hey!" Jason couldn't—didn't want to—believe that he'd imagined the statue. He reasoned it must have been taken down since his descent into the cleft at the beach. And what of the power outage that came after the earthquake? The streetlights illuminated around him, though the sun wouldn't be setting for another half hour. A streak of violet cascaded across the sky, and he remembered the gray-eyed girl biting him. He looked at both hands, but there was no sign of the wound he so clearly recalled Margot mending. If only all his wounds—even the emotional and psychological ones—could have vanished as quickly.

He had nothing to do now but return to the house and put everything behind him. It was easier to forget the disappearance of the statue and the wound than to strain his mind trying to conjure answers. It was like that in life, he reasoned. In life, so much time could be wasted trying to understand the causes of that which brings change or ruin. You can die suffering, upset, and vindictive of the misfortunes that have befallen you, or you can accept the pain—embrace it, welcome it—into the folds of your last living moments, however numerous or sparse they may be. Jason wished he'd had such clarity when Margot first left him. Maybe then he wouldn't have squandered away so many days in self-indulgent depression. There's no use dwelling in time lost, he thought, and he began walking again toward the house.

"Hey."

The voice was right behind him. He felt a hand on his shoulder and spun around. It was Margot's husband, Knox.

"Where is she?" Jason asked. He looked beyond Knox for Margot but didn't see her. "You should have found her by now."

"The boardwalk," Knox huffed. "Margot. Pregnant. Water just broke. Need help."

Jason remembered waking on the beach to find Margot sketching a landscape and their first daughter, Roxana, playing in the sand. Margot's belly had been swollen with a second child. The image was now as distant as a dream. He'd made love to Margot that night and awoke the next day to find she had long since given birth to the second girl, an implausible lapse in time. He remembered, after the gray-eyed girl had jumped into the cleft, sitting with Knox at its mouth, and Knox informing him that Margot was pregnant. Time is an illusion, Jason realized. What is before us is all that is real. And what was before him, whether he wanted it or not, was the husband of the up-to-this-point love of his life in desperate need.

"Tell me what to do," Jason said.

"Need a car," Knox said. "Pull up here and drive her to the Marina Del Rey hospital."

Jason winced, the name bringing back the steel-weighted punch he'd felt when the doctor told him they lost the baby.

He clenched his jaw. "Go to her. I'll meet you here in five. Quickly."

Knox nodded, and Jason saw a familiar fright in his eyes, the same he'd seen in his own when Margot had come to him the morning of the miscarriage.

"Something's wrong," she had said. "Something's wrong inside me."

Jason turned and sprinted toward the house. When he started the engine, the headlights automatically beamed; outside the car, twilight had begun to seize Venice in its serene, ever-mystical haze. When he first saw Knox and the dog on the beach, after slowly coming to, Jason had hoped he'd never again have to see Margot.

Maybe she won't remember me, he thought as he parked where he'd last seen Knox. Maybe she's not yet that far along.

He'd been idling near the boardwalk for five minutes when he saw Knox leading Margot, twice the size from when

Jason had last seen her, to the car. The dog was close behind her, her little four-legged protector. Jason got out and ran around to their side to open the back door. When she first saw him, she stopped and cocked her head as though Knox had not told her from whom they would be getting a ride.

"It's okay," said Knox. Jason averted his gaze from Margot's and caught a glimpse of her hand in Knox's. Jason felt a swift surge of envy trickle through him. He closed his eyes and squeezed the edge of the car door. When he opened his eyes, he watched Knox inch Margot down into the backseat using his hand to shield her from bumping her head. Jason didn't want to like Knox for being so gentle to Margot.

Once Margot was in the car, the dog climbed in beside her. Knox told her everything would be okay, and then he looked up to Jason. "Take care of her," he said. "Make sure she gets in safely. Make sure they take her immediately."

Jason demurred. "You're not coming?"

Margot grabbed Knox's wrist.

"Yes," she said. "You are. I know this is sudden, and it feels like we just met. But I need you there. Don't ask why. It just feels right, like you're meant to be there, too."

She held up her left hand, the back of it facing Knox. Jason saw Knox look at his own hand. They were comparing each other's wedding bands. Had they only just now resolved that they were married?

"Get in," Jason said.

Knox, his complexion now pale, nodded and followed Jason's command. Jason shut the door after him and returned to the driver's seat. He told Knox and Margot to buckle their seatbelts, and he started driving toward Windward Circle.

When they passed the house, he checked the rearview for any sign of recognition on Margot's face. What he saw was a bead of sweat forming on her stiff brow, her nostrils steadily expanding and contracting, and her eyes locked on her hands in Knox's.

She's no longer mine, Jason thought. I could have kept her on the other side, but I made the sacrifice.

An image of a child's drawing came to his mind—a snake. The last thing he saw in that other life. The pain he felt as the life drained from him until the shock overpowered the pain, and he was overcome with light. In the space between the light and the reemergence on the beach was the earthy smell after rainfall. He hadn't smelled it since Florida, and before he realized he was in Los Angeles, he thought he was in West Palm, still young enough to divert any misfortune that might have crossed him and Margot. When it set in that he was on Venice Beach, he first wondered if Margot was waiting for him at the house, perhaps painting a picture. He'd watched the waves, his muscles sore as if from lack of use, and let the memories wash up on the shore of his mind. Soon after the circumstances anchored, he looked up to see Knox and the dog, as if a bizarre twist of fate had led them to him. He thought then that life would continuously prove to be like the snake in the girl's drawing, wound up in an endless circle, eating and digesting itself until the end of time.

Even as he pulled into the emergency loop at the Marina Del Rey hospital, it was clear that God, or the cosmos, or whatever higher power orchestrated the chain of existence's events, wanted him to retread the waters of his past plights.

I will not drown, he thought. No matter how rough the tide may be, I will stay afloat.

Margot groaned from the backseat just as Jason parked the car.

"Are you okay?" Knox asked.

"Contraction," Margot said. "I'll be fine."

Jason turned the engine off, said, "Wait here. I'll go in for help and a wheelchair." He opened the door, but he stopped when he felt Margot's hand on his shoulder.

"Jason," she said. "I know how hard this must be. I know everything got messed up. Despite all of it. Thank you."

He could barely look at her except out of the corner of his eye. Frozen in place, he felt a sudden rush of shame and guilt and longing, which grew hot inside him, producing involuntary tears. He craned his neck to hide this and, with a shaky voice, said, "I'm happy to help you. Really. No trouble at all."

Before she could say any more, Jason put his feet to the pavement, shut the door, and started briskly toward the hospital's entrance. When he got to the front desk, the receptionist looked up glaringly from her computer screen. He'd seen her before, but it was obvious from her overworked gaze that he was a stranger in her eyes.

"How can I help you?" she asked. "What is your emergency?"

"Outside," Jason said. "A woman is in labor. A friend of mine."

Jason walked the dog around the hospital a dozen times, trying to forget, or at least ignore, the fact that, inside, in some room, Margot was about to give birth to another man's child. Although he had quit a long time ago, he bummed a cigarette from a guy who sat chain-smoking outside the ER.

"Handsome dog," the guy said.

"It's not mine," Jason said.

"I saw you wheeling in a pregnant woman. Congratulations."

"Not mine, either. She's just a friend."

Jason took a long drag on the cigarette and sensed the dog's eyes on him as if being judged.

The guy exhaled a smoke ring. "My girl's up there right now pushing out our baby boy. Been damn near sixteen hours. I about passed out, so I figured I'd come down here for some air."

"Congratulations," Jason said, and he stuffed the butt of his cigarette into the receptacle. "I'll pray for your baby's health, and your wife's." Jason hadn't prayed since his last visit to the Marina Del Rey hospital, and he hadn't prayed for several years before that. He no longer knew if he believed in the power of prayer.

"Oh, she's not my wife. We're not married." The guy chortled and lit another cigarette. "At least not yet, anyway. Who knows if marriage even matters anymore. But I'll tell you what—I'm going to be a damn great daddy to that child. You got any of your own?"

Jason tightly wrapped the dog's leash around his wrist to briefly cut off the circulation. He thought of Roxana and Tiffany. He wanted to ask for a second cigarette but decided against it.

"No," Jason said. "At least not yet, anyway."

The guy smiled. "Well, let me tell you. It's the best feeling in the world."

Jason relieved the leash from his wrist. He felt the blood stream back into his fingers.

"I bet," he said. "Take care."

"You do the same. And I'll say a prayer for your friend's health, and her baby's."

"Please do," Jason said. He gave the dog's leash a gentle tug and started walking toward the parking garage.

He had told Knox he would look after the dog while they were inside, for however long it took. He bought a bottle of water from a vending machine outside and poured some into the dog's mouth. Earlier, he'd bought a sandwich from the hospital cafeteria and gave the dog the turkey from it. The dog looked up at Jason calmly, its tongue lapping at the slow stream of water. Jason scratched behind the dog's ears and ran his hand along its shiny yellow coat.

"Good boy," Jason said.

The dog wagged its tail and Jason led it to the parking garage elevator. He pushed the button for the topmost level and, when he and the dog got out, it was as if the gossamery clouds drifting across the night sky were within arm's reach. At the north-facing ledge of the garage, he saw in the distance lights illuminating the different neighborhoods of West LA—Venice, Santa Monica, Century City. He wondered what this view would have looked like, how dark and vacuous it would have appeared during the blackout—if there had even been a blackout. He wondered if he should have asked the chain-smoker if he recalled an earthquake or power outage recently. Some questions are better left unanswered, Jason figured. Some things cannot be determined by logic.

32

IT WAS ALL happening so fast. As soon as Knox and Jason had wheeled Margot inside, the nurses took Margot through a set of large doors down a bright hallway. The receptionist at the front desk looked at him and said, "Are you the father? Don't worry. We're going to take great care of your wife. Take these papers and fill them out as soon as possible. You can follow the nurse to your wife's room."

Knox took the stack of files and gulped. "Just need a minute," he said. He looked around for somewhere to sit.

The receptionist gave him a sidelong glance and nudged her head toward a hallway on her left. "You can go sit in the waiting area."

He nodded and went to take a moment's reprieve with the spouses, family members, and friends of other patients. He still couldn't face Margot and this child. Not yet. His eyes fell toward the papers in his lap. A needed distraction. Could it help him remember? With the pen in his hand, he felt a debilitating shock overcome him. He didn't know where to begin. Around him, he saw people coming and going through the set of large doors, each with a sense of urgency and purpose. All he heard was the pounding of his heart.

Focus, he thought. She needs you.

Your wife needs you.

Your child needs you.

He thought about what Margot said to him:

'I know this is sudden, and it feels like we just met. But I need you there. Don't ask why. It just feels right, like you're meant to be there, too.'

How could it be that he couldn't remember his own pregnant wife upon seeing her? How could it be that she couldn't remember him? Perhaps they had been concussed. It seemed Lane was the only one to remember anything. It had been Lane who led him to Jason.

Jason, who told him: 'There's nothing I can tell you that you don't already know.'

In Jason's car, while holding Margot and looking at her pregnant belly, Knox saw a different version of himself, one who was a father. Feeling the warmth of Margot's hand, the rhythm of her pulse, and possibly that of the baby's, made Knox accept the reality in front of him. Margot had taken his hand and pressed his palm against the flesh of her belly. Inside her, within her, the baby moved. Knox then feared, blood rushing to his face, that this reality, like the one dissipating from his memory, would be swept out from under him.

The rush of emotion made the paperwork easier. Knox put the pen to paper and, suddenly, all of the information flowed out of him: names, dates, insurance, telephone numbers. It was all stored in his brain, somewhere down a previously inaccessible chamber of memory. When he finished, he returned the stack to the receptionist and asked, "Can you please take me to my wife now?" A nurse led him to the corridor where they had taken Margot, its bright lights strong enough to make him wince.

As soon as they arrived at Margot's room, Knox faltered at the sight of her in the hospital bed and changed into a delivery gown. She lay with her legs bent, both hands on her belly, an IV taped to her forearm. The nurse led him past a bassinet and pointed at the monitor to which Margot was connected.

"She's just under five minutes between contractions," the nurse said, showing Knox the rising and falling line on the monitor.

"I opted for an intrathecal," Margot said with a shrug of her shoulders. "They don't advise an epidural this late. But it will numb me to most of the pain."

"Probably for the best," Knox said.

"I'm surprised you didn't have a birth plan." The nurse continued reading the monitor and jotted notes onto a clipboard. "But they're not for everyone, I guess."

When the nurse left the room, Margot took Knox's hand and squeezed it. Though her face was latent, Knox knew she was doing her best to conceal the pain.

"You don't have to hide it," he said. "It's no use. Soon the drugs will kick in. As a matter of fact, you think I could score some?"

Margot smiled, and the way her face lit up at his dumb joke reminded him of mornings with her in bed.

"If you need to lie down, there's a gigantic tub in the bathroom."

Knox laughed, and he habitually leaned in to kiss Margot's sweaty forehead. When he pulled back, they shared a glance that asked, 'Why does it feel like the first time, yet also the millionth?'

"There is a flutter of butterflies inside me," he said, the onset of tears making his jaw tremble. "And I just know, at my core, from the bottom of my heart, that I love you completely, Margot."

She squeezed his hand more tightly.

"I have no doubt," she said, "that I have loved you for a long time, and that my love for you is deeper than oceans."

He felt a tear hit his cheek.

"Faster than rivers," he said.

"Stronger than waterfalls."

They looked into each other's eyes. Knox stroked her face and understood, finally, all that had to happen to bring them to this point. Each misstep. Each loss. Each sacrifice.

33

MARGOT HEARD THE words "fetal monitoring strips."

Margot heard the words "abnormal heart tracings."

Margot asked what was wrong, but nobody answered her.

"Hello? I'm the one delivering this baby!"

The obstetrician came around to her and explained the nuchal cord.

The obstetrician suggested an emergency C-section.

"Make it simple," Margot demanded. "Tell me plainly what is wrong with my baby."

"The umbilical cord," the obstetrician said, "is wrapped around its neck. There is a significant decrease in the flow of oxygen-rich blood to the brain. We must act now."

The obstetrician, one of the nurses, and Knox rolled Margot onto her back.

"You need to give consent," Knox said.

Margot felt she was about to choke.

"You have my consent."

The medical staff began to roll her out of the room and down the bright corridor. Knox stayed by her side, holding her hand.

"Everything is going to be okay," he assured.

She nodded.

"I don't want to lose another baby."

Knox shook his head.

"You won't."

In the operating room, nurses draped a blue screen around her to sterilize the incision site. A catheter was inserted into her bladder.

She saw white lights and Knox's silhouette.

And then pain. Hot pain, despite the intrathecal.

They told her they were cleaning her abdomen.

They put an oxygen mask over her nose and mouth.

Knox said, "Don't worry. Everything will be okay."

She wanted to believe him.

Please, she thought.

Let my baby be okay.

Let this baby be okay.

She heard the doctor say an incision was being made through the uterus.

She felt pressure and tugging and pulling.

"Here we go," someone said. "We have a head."

"Wrapped around four times," someone said.

"Alright, one at a time."

Margot felt a weight upon her.

She felt Knox's hands steadying her.

She heard the baby's cries.

"She's beautiful," someone said. "She's perfect."

She.

Her baby was here.

Her baby girl.

ꟷ

In the recovery ward, Margot held her baby, and Knox held Margot. In a few moments, the midwife would enter and help them with the breastfeeding. Margot kept the baby's tufts of blonde hair to her lips, indulging in its earthy smell. The baby was sound asleep, the only noise her little, periodic up-and-down breaths.

"I never knew I could love something this much," Knox whispered.

"Neither did I."

"Do you have any idea what you want to name her?"

Margot traced her fingers along the baby's neckline.

So close the baby had come to not being here at all.

So close she and Knox had come to losing everything.

Knox caressed the baby's cheek.

They sat in the recovery room, waiting for the midwife, listening to the child's soft squeaks, when the overhead lights flickered.

"What was that?" asked Margot.

The floor suddenly started to shake.

"Tremor," said Knox.

He wrapped his arms around Margot and the baby and used his torso to shield them.

The room went still, but Margot waited for something more.

The lights flickered again, and the recovery ward fell dark.

EPILOGUE

PENELOPE

Dear Mom and Dad,

Happy Anniversary.

Every year around this time, I can't help thinking about how grateful I am.

Remember how close I came?

So close to not existing.

I often think about the choices you made.

All of those that led to me.

Each step—one perfect step after another—had to be taken just so for me to be here. Mine is a life intricately woven.

You've told me the stories of how you lost me.

You've tried to explain how you never lost me.

You've taught me the myth, which I now believe like scripture: Persephone's mercy, and the importance of never looking back.

It has taken me so much time to understand how all of my choices also led to you.

Everything I decide to do.

Everything I decide against.

It sounds backward, I know—the old conundrum of the chicken and the egg.

Which came first?

Was it you, or was it me?

I still have the dreams.

I dream of myself as other people.

Rather, I dream of myself living different lives.

There's me. There's you. There are other people, and we all keep cycling through one another's lives.

Sometimes I wake and feel as though I'm still dreaming.

It grows difficult to tell them apart.

The dreams and the real.

But there is something in the unknowing that gives me comfort.

Something in the reveries that tethers me to reality.

The anchor of love.

In all our many lives, in all our roles to play, it is love—in all its manifestations—that binds us.

It is true that love begets pain.

As pain begets more pain.

And so it is: Love and pain interwoven endlessly.

A stitch so simple, so elegant in its design, we hardly notice the suture to the wound.

ACKNOWLEDGMENTS

WRITING CAN BE a lonesome process. The following folks have made it less so:

Many thanks to Charlie Franco and the rest of the team at Montag Press for making this novel a reality. To Amit Dey: Thank you for your endless patience and your sleek designs. To Kate Sargeant: Your insights and thoughts about this manuscript brought the book to new heights; I am convinced there is no other person who would have been more suited to edit this novel than you.

Thank you to the writers and teachers who helped guide me: Alma Luz Villanueva, Alistair McCartney, Francesca Lia Block, Peter Selgin, Jim Krusoe, Steve Heller, Brad Kessler, Gary Phillips, Donald Morrill, Jane Bradley (may you rest in peace), and Kyle Minor. Thank you to my early readers/workshop mates who gave notes on this manuscript: Taj Rauf, Jessica O'Dwyer, Michelle Templeton, Katelyn Keating, Jasper Henderson, Stephanie Teasley, Mark Valley, and Jahzerah Brooks. Thank you to Alex Thurnher, Jesus Sierra, Tim Cummings, Mireya Vela, Andrea Auten, Andre Hardy, Stephen Desjarlais, Katy Avila, Ari Rosenschein, Meg Gaertner, Kelly Hobkirk, Vibiana Aparacio, Anna Vangala Jones, Jane-Rebecca Cannarella, Ken Pienkos, Lisa Lepore,

Kim Sabin, Deidre Baird, and so many other great friends and writers from Antioch University Los Angeles.

A million thank yous are in order to the incredible writers who have supported this novel and my story collection, *The Reincarnations*: Donald Ray Pollock, Tiffany Quay Tyson, Andromeda Romano-Lax, Ben Loory, Sequoia Nagamatsu, Gayle Brandeis, J.D. Scott, Christopher Clancy, Sean Kinch, Pedro Ponce, Bradley Sides, Jeff Vande Zande, Michael B. Tager, Paul D. Miller, and more.

To those who have long been in my corner—thank you: Chavar Dontae, Carrie Bird, Allison Fiscus, Jeannie Keys, Katie Kudas, Maggie Smith, anyone who worked with me at the Barnes & Noble in the Shops at Fallen Timbers or The Grove in Los Angeles, and many others.

To The Porch, Keep St. Pete Lit, Wordier Than Thou, the Ohioana Library Association, Book Soup, Skylight Books, and other stellar organizations: Thank you for having me.

To my family: Dad, Tracy & Rich, Dawn, Cathy (rest in peace), Dustin, Amanda, Matthew, Shannon, the New York and Florida clans, the entire Pennsylvania clan, the Johnsons—I love you all more than you know.

Thank you, Alexi, for your endless support and belief. I am certain you are at the center of each and every alternate universe I may inhabit.

Thank you, reader, for lending your imagination to these words.

Thank you, God, for everything.

AUTHOR BIO

NATHAN ELIAS is the author of *The Reincarnations: Stories*. He holds an MFA in Creative Writing from Antioch University Los Angeles, his writing has been nominated for the Pushcart Prize and Best Microfiction, and he was a finalist of *The Saturday Evening Post* 2020 Great American Fiction Contest. His short fiction, poetry, essays, and book reviews have appeared in publications such as *PANK*, *Entropy*, *Hobart*, *Pithead Chapel*, and *Barnstorm*. He lives in Nashville, Tennessee with his wife and rescue dog. *Coil Quake Rift* is his debut novel.

Made in the USA
Monee, IL
26 September 2022

14613779R00163